Praise for Jessica James' Books

"Very engaging. Hard to put down." — BILLY ALLMON, U.S. Navy SEAL (Retired)

"Sweetly sentimental and moving… An endearing page-turner." — PUBLISHERS WEEKLY

"A tapestry of emotion deeply set inside the bravest of Americans: the soldier." — MILITARY WRITERS SOCIETY of AMERICA

"Reminds me of *American Sniper* and *Lone Survivor*, but accompanied with a beautiful and epic love story that is completely unforgettable." — LAUREN HOFF, United States Air Force

"A heart-rending, white-knuckle journey into the courageous lives of our nation's heroes. Shows us the meaning of commitment—to country, and to love." — JOCELYN GREEN, Award-winning author

Other Books by Jessica James

Romantic Suspense
DEAD LINE (Book 1 Phantom Force Tactical)
FINE LINE (Book 2 Phantom Force Tactical)
FRONT LINE (Book 3 Phantom Force Tactical)

Meant To Be: A Novel of Honor and Duty

Historical Fiction
The Lion of the South

Noble Cause (Book 1 Heroes Through History)
(An alternative ending to Shades of Gray)

Above and Beyond (Book 2 Heroes Through History)
Liberty and Destiny (Book 3 Heroes Through History)

Shades of Gray: A Novel of the Civil War in Virginia

Non-Fiction
The Gray Ghost of Civil War Virginia: John Singleton Mosby
From the Heart: Love Stories and Letters from the Civil War

www.jessicajamesbooks.com

JESSICA JAMES
HONOR COURAGE LOVE

Protecting Ashley

A Phantom Force Tactical Novel (Book 4)

Jessica James

#WarriorReader

Chapter 1

—

"You've got to be kidding me."

Jarrod "Lance" Landis placed both hands on his boss's desk and leaned forward to look him in the eye. "If I wanted to be a bodyguard, I sure as hell wouldn't be working for Phantom Force Tactical."

"I know. I know." Nicholas "Colt" Colton leaned back in his high-backed leather chair with his arms crossed. "But it's only for a week."

"A *day* would be too long." Lance paced in front of the desk a moment. "An *hour* would be—"

"Is that a *no?*"

"I didn't say that." Lance stopped walking. "But why me?" He reclined into a chair near the desk and leaned forward, elbows on his knees, hands clasped. "I mean, level with me. Am I on your shit list already or something? Why can't someone else do it?"

"Because you're the NFG," Colt replied calmly. "End of conversation."

Lance took a deep breath and let it out slowly. Well, he had him there. Good to know it wasn't anything personal, but it still stung. Sure, he was the New F-ing Guy at this particular security agency, but he'd been deployed to some of the most dangerous locations in the world during his ten years of special operations service. The job he was being requested to perform was more like a rent-a-cop or private bodyguard position. No one else in the company would want it, and Colt probably wouldn't dream of asking any of them. The guys at Phantom Force Tactical were some of the most respected, well trained, bad-ass former military men in the world.

Lance stared vacantly at the ceiling as he began to accept that Colt was right. This job *had* to go to the NFG. How would it look to the guys who'd been with the agency for dozens of years if the one hired six weeks ago, walked in and chose which ops he'd accept? He had to shrug it off, take the gig, and work his way up the ladder like everyone else had. Truthfully, he was flattered—honored—to have received the call to be a part of this team in the first place. Everyone in the business looked at Phantom Force as one of the top agencies in the world—and being given the opportunity to sit down and have this conversation with the legendary Nick Colton was a privilege in and of itself.

Lance raked a hand through his dark hair. "Okay. What's the backstory?" The excitement he'd felt this morning at getting the call for his first real solo op with Phantom Force seeped out of him as the reality of the situation sank in.

Colt didn't gloat or show any emotion as he pulled a folder out from under a pile and handed it across the desk.

Lance groaned when he opened it. Taped to the inside was a photo of a young woman in a sparkling full-length gown, waving toward the camera. She appeared to be attending a red-carpet event or perhaps a charity function. A matching diamond necklace and bracelet reflected the lights surrounding her so that the entire figure appeared to sparkle. A smile, made for cameras, was highlighted by shiny red lips that magnified the overall appearance of perfection.

"Striking, isn't she?"

Lance looked up from the picture. "Not exactly what I was thinking."

"Really? What were you thinking?" Colt sat back in his chair with half a smile on his face, his brows raised questioningly.

"I was thinking that I'm going to have to deal with an obscenely rich, hopelessly spoiled, and probably terribly bad-tempered prima donna."

"Why do you say that?"

"Look at her." Lance held the picture up. "She's beautiful. Apparently, filthy rich. Accustomed to being waited on and served." Lance's attention went back to the other paperwork in the folder.

"Well at least you can admit she's good looking." Colt frowned. "I was beginning to wonder..."

Lance grunted in reply, and continued reading. "Says here her father is Franklin Hathaway." He looked up. "*The* Franklin Hathaway? The Hollywood producer?"

"That's the one."

"I think I read somewhere that he died."

"About a year ago." Colt's smile disappeared, and his expression turned grim. "He had just turned fifty."

"What happened?"

"Car accident...they say."

Lance heard the sarcasm in his voice, but he was so intent

on scanning the file, he didn't question it.

"I don't see any siblings." Lance's eyes darted up. "She's an only child?"

Colt nodded. "Her mother died when she was three."

"Great." Lance let out his breath. "So she inherited the entire Hathaway fortune."

"You make it sound like that's a bad thing."

"I'm just saying, it means she's never worked a day in her life. Never struggled."

"I wouldn't assume too much if I were you." Colt tapped his pencil on the desk, and appeared a little irritated.

Again, Lance heard the tone, but let it go. Instead, he studied Colt in silence for a few moments. "Level with me. What's up with this? It's not the kind of op that Phantom Force usually takes on."

"You're right about that." Colt's steady gaze locked on his. "But it's…complicated."

Lance's brow creased with confusion. "Meaning?"

"Someone called in a favor."

"Hmm. Must be a pretty close friend and a pretty big favor."

"That's right."

Lance knew he wouldn't get anything more out of Colt on that topic. He was the type of man who never gave out any more information than was absolutely necessary, and was a master at keeping things secret. Maybe that's why he was so popular, and why anyone worth his salt in private security wanted to be a part of his team.

Lance leaned back in his chair and exhaled. "Okay, lay this

all out for me. What does this involve exactly?"

"Well, ever since her father died, she's pretty much become a recluse." Colt's gaze moved to somewhere over Lance's shoulder. "She didn't take it well."

"Her father's death, you mean?"

Colt nodded as Lance's attention went back to the file. "But it says here she's going to be traveling again."

"That's right." Colt nodded. "And one of her father's old friends wants someone to keep an eye on her."

"And that *old friend* is also an old friend of yours?"

Colt didn't answer, letting Lance know he'd pushed too far and was asking too many questions. He tried to change the subject. "She looks like she's old enough to take care of herself to me." Lance stared at the photo again. "Probably has a whole entourage of people with her at all times. Can't they babysit her?"

"It's not babysitting." Colt's voice grew a bit more emotional. "This *is* a legitimate security mission." He leaned forward with an intent look on his face after a prolonged silence. "I know it sucks. I know it's not your type of op. But once it's done, I'll owe you one."

Lance's head jerked toward him. "What does that mean exactly?"

"When you get back, I'll give you something extra juicy."

A slight smile twitched at the corner of Lance's mouth. In "Colt talk," extra juicy meant something extra dangerous, and that suited him just fine. If Lance had to do this one little thing in order to win this man's esteem, he would do it and give it his all.

Colt and his business partner had started Phantom Force Tactical less than a decade ago, but it was already one of the most renowned names in the business. Everyone in this line of work had heard about the exploits of Colt and his partner Blake Madison. Both former Navy SEALs, they had records of distinction both on and off the battlefield. After getting severely injured in a secret operation, Blake had left the service and become a homicide detective. He and Colt later fulfilled a life-long dream by starting the company.

"Must be a pretty big favor someone is calling in."

A slight nod of the head was Colt's only reply. This was a man whose entire adult life had consisted of hair's-breadth escapes and some of the most dangerous missions ever undertaken. Even after leaving the service, Colt had eagerly volunteered for ops that other men said couldn't be done. In his younger years, he'd traveled from one end of the globe to another, meeting royalty and heads of state, and forming alliances with the top security agencies of allied countries. There was no one of any diplomatic importance he didn't know. It wasn't hard to conceive that a lot of people in high places owed Colt favors—but it had never occurred to Lance that Colt *owed* a few too.

"Okay. I'm in."

"Great." Colt dug through another pile of papers on his desk and pulled out a folder. "Here are your travel arrangements and a plane ticket. You leave tomorrow."

Again, Lance's head jerked up. "How'd you know I was going to say *yes?*"

Colt's eyes locked on his. "I know my guys."

Chapter 2

L ance was beginning to doubt the accuracy of his GPS, even though it was better than most on the market. It seemed like he was getting further and further away from civilization, but he still hadn't reached his turnoff. Rounding a sharp turn, he had to steer hard to the right to keep from hitting a car that was in his lane.

"Slow down, buddy." By the time he'd gotten his vehicle under control and shifted his gaze to the rear-view mirror, the car was gone. But the driver's face was imprinted in his mind, and the vehicle—a plain white van—was stamped in his memory.

Just a few seconds later, Lance's GPS began to signal for a right-hand turn. He drove alongside an ornate wrought-iron fence for a short distance, then turned into the main entrance that was flanked by two stone pillars and an impressive-looking gate. Each pillar had a large "H" emblazoned on the front, verifying he was at the right place. Maneuvering his truck close to the touchpad, he shifted his foot to the brake as he pulled a crumpled piece of paper from his back pocket and squinted at the numbers.

It occurred to Lance that this was a strange way to arrive for a meeting, but he hadn't questioned it until now. Was there a reason Colt had given him the gate's code instead of just having him go through the Hathaway security team? He looked around. Actually, he didn't see any security. Not humans anyway. There was a camera attached to the small guardhouse, but the building itself was empty.

As soon as the numbers were tapped in, the huge gates began to move. *That was easy*, he thought, as he stepped on the accelerator. *But does anyone know I'm coming?*

The more he thought about it, the more he began to think this whole operation was some type of training exercise for Phantom Force, rather than a legitimate mission. He wouldn't put it past Colt to test all of his recruits this way—send them on a supposedly easy op and then throw strange situations at them to see how they reacted. He speculated that perhaps he would be watched and graded on how well he performed. He'd better stay on his toes…and play nice. He frowned. Playing nice with a spoiled brat was going to test his skills to their breaking limit. *Good way to train the new guy, Colt.*

Lance's head moved on a swivel now as he proceeded up the winding, brick-paved drive. Being aware of his surroundings was part of his job, but today, it was more of a case of not believing what he was seeing.

The trees lining the road were magnificent, their limbs creating a natural canopy of green. When he ascended a hill and came out of the tunnel formed by foliage, the view was breathtaking. Nothing but rolling hills and green fields as far as the eye could see—until the house came into view.

Holy cow.

Lance felt like he was pulling up to the front of a movie set as he steered his truck around the circular drive. Except for the gold three-tiered fountain that threw sparkling water into the air, it appeared he was sitting in front of the mansion from *Gone with the Wind*. A sea of flowers surrounded the fountain, spreading out in wave after wave of color. His attention moved to the wide, welcoming porch that appeared to be made of marble. He tilted his head back to take in the four large pillars that graced the front of the home. Yep. Marble, too.

Lance took a deep breath and exited the truck. He began to wonder if he was underdressed in his simple blazer and jeans. *Too late to worry about it now.* His boots made a gentle clicking sound as he crossed the huge landing and rang the doorbell. It didn't take long for a man dressed in formal attire to open the door.

"May I help you?" His gaze swept over Lance's shoulder and he leaned forward a little to gaze out the door, as if not quite sure how this stranger had gotten through the gate.

"Good morning. I'm here to see Ms. Hathaway."

The man looked even more surprised. "Do you have an appointment, sir?"

Lance wasn't sure how to answer that. Colt had given him the directions, the security code, and told him what time to arrive. He assumed his boss had informed the client he was coming—but he should have known better than to assume anything with Colt. "I'm, uh, not sure."

The man stared at Lance a moment, and then shook his head. "And your name, sir?"

"Jarrod Landis." He pulled out his official ID and showed the man.

"Oh, yes." The man seemed to remember hearing the name. "Very well. I'll see if I can *find* her." He still seemed a bit unsure about inviting Lance in, but after assessing him a moment, opened the door and motioned for him to enter with his hand. "Wait here." He then turned and strode toward a massive door at the end of the hall, mumbling as he walked, suggesting by his tone that locating the mistress of the large house would be no easy task.

Lance stood in the large foyer, and waited, his eyes ever busy. He'd noticed another security camera on the porch, but didn't see any in here. The entryway was large, with a black and white checkerboard floor and two white pillars that stood beneath an archway into the next room. In front of each pillar stood small tables with fresh bouquets of flowers spilling out over the vases. Off to his right was an elaborate curving staircase that ascended to the second floor.

Just as Lance's gaze landed on a sparkling crystal chandelier hanging over the stairway, the clamor of footsteps and the sound of humming reached his ears. The sight of feet descending the stairs two at a time came into view shortly thereafter.

Raising his gaze a little more, he took in a pair of torn and ragged jeans that were half in and half out of a pair of untied work boots. A flannel shirt appeared next—followed by the appearance of wavy hair bouncing off the shoulders of a young woman. When the figure saw him, she stopped abruptly. "Garth, sit."

Lance's eyes moved to the German shepherd that had been following just behind her. The dog appeared watchful and vigilant, but obeyed the order, and sat on the step just behind her.

"Who are you?" The young woman eyed him suspiciously.

"Jarrod Landis. I'm here to meet Ms. Hathaway." Lance took in the tousled hair and the tattered jeans, and wondered who this creature was and why she was here.

"For what?"

"If you'll direct me to Ms. Hathaway, I'll explain all of that."

He watched a curtain of annoyance descend upon her features, followed by obvious forced calmness that comes from lots of practice. "There must have been a mix-up of some sort. Who sent you?"

Lance hesitated to respond, not sure if that was information he was supposed to divulge. Where in the hell was the Hathaway lady? And why was this stable girl acting like a bodyguard? Maybe *she* should be the one given the job of protecting the asset. *Damn you, Colt. What did you get me into?*

The woman straightened up menacingly and crossed her arms over her chest. But before she had time to reveal what was on her mind, the wooden door at the end of the hall opened and the man Lance had met earlier hurried through, slightly out of breath. He followed Lance's gaze to the figure on the stairs, and stopped. "Oh. I see you've found her."

Lance stood still, his gaze bouncing from one to the other like he was watching a tennis ball during a high-stakes match. The tension in the room became palpable, and his surprise could not have been more complete.

"Why is he here, Stan?" the young woman moved her hands

to her hips. Her blue eyes, which had been wide and almond-shaped, were now mere slits as she stared at the nervous and fidgety man who had opened the door and let this stranger in.

"I-I'm not sure. I think maybe…perhaps—"

Her eyes darted back to Lance and her look was direct. She had apparently decided to bypass the middleman and ask him directly. "Why are you here?"

Lance had never been known for his patience, and what little he possessed had vanished during his idle time in the foyer. The speculation that this was Colt's idea of a joke on the new guy was beginning to look more conclusive. He suppressed the urge to look again for a camera—a hidden one—and imagined the guys back at Phantom Force Tactical having a good laugh if they were watching his reaction at this moment. Maybe he should just end this right here and now.

But instead of turning and walking back out the door, as his instinct told him to do, Lance decided to play along. Damned if he was going to roll over and give in—practical joke or not. He pretended that *he* was the one in control of the situation. "I would tell you if I could, but I can't so I won't."

A quick flash of anger replaced the look of suspicion, followed immediately by an expression of complete annoyance. She crossed her arms and tilted her head. "Who did you say you worked for?"

"I don't know what that has to do with anything," Lance replied elusively.

"Really? How'd you get through the security gate?"

In his line of work, Lance knew that every op was different. There was no way to predict what any given day would bring, which was one of the reasons he loved this business so much. The variability and uniqueness of each situation required his mind to be in constant motion and his body to continually endure intensive training. Yet, never had he imagined that he would be standing in a foyer arguing with a client. In past experiences, they *wanted* his help and expertise. His gaze darted over to the man she'd called Stan, who seemed equally unsure of what to do.

"Perhaps you should take Mr. Landis into the library and discuss this in private," he said, looking at the woman hopefully.

The woman's laser-like gaze remained focused on Lance. "You were sent to keep an eye on me. Security." The words were not posed as a question, but rather an imperial command for him to confirm her supposition.

Lance didn't want to appear taken aback, but it was hard to look into those eyes. He gave a curt nod of confirmation. "If you are Ms. Hathaway." He still couldn't believe the woman in front of him was the glamorous icon he'd seen in the photos. Then again, the eyes *were* the same, which is to say, stunning. A brilliant blue, they were like deep pools of temptation that made you want to fall in.

When Lance had seen the photos, he'd assumed they'd been enhanced. Now he could see that airbrushing the pictures wasn't necessary. She was captivating even without makeup or fancy clothes.

He watched her descend the remaining stairs, the dog at her side sniffing Lance as it passed.

"Follow me."

There was no hesitation or questioning in her voice. She had just given him a command.

Lance glanced back at Stan before following the woman and the dog. The man simply shrugged and nodded, but his eyes carried a look of relief that seemed to imply he was glad they were retiring to another room.

Chapter 3

Ashley Hathaway stood at a window with her back to Lance when he entered. "I don't like surprises," she said, not bothering to turn around.

"I'm sorry, Miss Hathaway. I was under the impression that someone had contacted you and arranged a meeting."

He heard her take a long drawn out sigh, as she seemed to be deep in thought. "Did Rad send you?"

"Rad?"

She turned around, her hands in her pockets. "He's retired military... a good friend of my father's." Her voice broke slightly. "*Was* a good friend."

"No. I don't know a Rad." But as soon as Lance said the words, it all started to fall into place. He remembered Colt once saying that if there was one person he'd like to have on his team, it was Rad—a retired military man who'd gone into private security later in life. Maybe it *was* Rad who'd set this up. It wouldn't be inconceivable that Rad had done some off-the-books work for Colt—work that no one else had the skills, ability, or connections to do.

"I don't know him personally..." Lance tried to clarify his response, "but that doesn't mean Rad wasn't the one to arrange this. Guys in my line of work are..."

"Like brothers," she finished for him.

Lance studied the reflective look on her face. That wasn't what he was going to say, but it was true, so he nodded his head.

"So you just admitted that you're in the security business," she said, turning back to the window. "That's a start."

Lance didn't like having the tables turned on him, especially by someone he'd just met—and particularly not by a stunningly beautiful female. The women he usually came into contact with were sitting on a barstool waiting for a man to buy them a drink—and for whatever followed.

"Yes. We've established that," he said, trying to regain control of the conversation. "Now it's your turn."

"My turn?" She gazed at him over her shoulder.

"Tell me what's going on here. Apparently you're in need of security."

"Didn't your boss tell you all of that?"

At his silence, she turned all the way around. Her lips lifted into a smile and her eyes twinkled with merriment. "So you were roped into this? Unaware of what you were getting into? What are you, the new guy or something?"

Dammit. Why did she keep asking him questions in a way that made them awkward to answer?

When his answer was not forthcoming, she laughed out loud. "I know Uncle Rad wields a lot of power, but this takes the cake."

Lance cocked his head. "*Uncle* Rad? This Rad dude is your *uncle*?"

"Not really." She let her breath out as she walked to a cluster of chairs. "But he was like an uncle to me. My father has a foundation for veterans, and met Rad way back when he was still a SEAL. Rad went through some tough times getting over a mission that killed two—" She stopped abruptly and studied Lance with a puzzled look on her face. "Your boss didn't tell you any of this?"

Lance put his hand on his temples and squeezed. Colt hadn't divulged much information, but what *she* had just told him helped put things into place. If Rad had been a SEAL, then he and Colt probably went way back. The SEAL family was relatively small. Everyone knew everyone—or at least knew *of* everyone.

Now that he thought about it, Lance *did* remember hearing about the guy named Rad. Michael Radcliff was his name. He'd led the mission that took down a top-tier terrorist in Afghanistan and then rescued a hostage. Almost lost a leg in the process, if memory served.

Rad—and many of the others who served during that period—were now like living legends to those of Lance's era. The feats of daring and heroism of the older generation of SEALs were so admirable and courageous that it kept the newer classes on their toes. They were always striving to equal the accomplishments of those who came before.

When Lance looked at Ashley again, she seemed to have a relieved look on her face, as if she was thankful he hadn't been told very much. Lance inadvertently dropped his gaze down to her faded jeans and boots, before catching himself and bringing his eyes up to her face.

"What's wrong?" Another slight smile flashed. "This isn't what you were expecting?" She held her hands out to display her attire more fully.

Lance tried not to stare. No makeup. Ripped jeans. Men's boots. Yet the woman was simply breathtaking. He cleared his throat. "Let's just say that isn't how you were dressed in the file photo I received."

"Or the YouTube videos you watched?" She tilted her head to the side, and stared at him with her blue eyes sparkling intensely.

Lance stood silently as he tried to figure out how to respond without admitting that he had indeed watched a video or two. Of course, he'd done a little research. Who wouldn't have? He'd been given so little background information, he'd wanted to see what he was getting into.

"I see." She put an exquisitely manicured finger under her chin, and turned back toward the large window that looked out over a magnificent garden. Water from another fountain sparkled like a million diamonds as it was thrown high into the air, and caught the rays of the sun.

Lance decided it was time to take control of the meeting. He needed to salvage something from his time spent here. He'd been in the house for almost a half hour, and didn't know anything more than when he'd first arrived. Actually, he knew even less, because he had more questions *now* than before.

He closed the gap between them. "Since we've not really been introduced…" He held out his hand. "I'm Jarrod Landis. Everyone calls me Lance."

She turned around, stared into his eyes a moment before lowering her gaze to his hand. "Ashley Hathaway," she finally said, grasping it. "Pleased to meet you, Lance."

Lance was a little shocked by the strength of her grip, and realized once again that he'd made an assumption. This wasn't the soft and pliable "Hollywood handshake" that he'd expected from someone who spent hours at meet-and-greet events. It was firm and businesslike, revealing a woman who was both confident and competent.

"Now let's get down to business. Tell me what's going on."

Instead of answering, she strolled over to a cabinet, opened the door, and bent down to look inside "Something to drink? I can have Stan bring coffee or tea."

"No, I'm good." He wondered why she was stalling.

She shrugged and grabbed a bottle of water, then sat down, crossing her legs in a graceful, ladylike manner. Despite her attire, it was clear that manners and appearances had been ingrained in her as a child. She looked as prim and proper as if she were at a party, sipping tea and passing the time with royalty. "What exactly does my file say?"

Her long lashes shadowed her cheeks as she looked down to open the bottle of water, but when she raised her head to meet his gaze, the look was intense.

Lance's brow creased as he shot her a bewildered look. "What do you mean?"

"Whoever your boss is gave you a file. Right? I'm curious. What did it say?"

Lance tried to control the lump that had formed in his throat so he wouldn't be seen swallowing it. Most clients didn't really know about—or at least *think* about—the fact that a security team had gathered background material on them. Sometimes it could be a pretty massive compilation of everything about the person—from the time they went to bed, to where they went and when throughout the day. He tried to act as businesslike and casual as she. "Like I said before, not much. Just the basics."

"Such as?"

"Look, I don't see how that's any of your business."

"It's a file on me and it's none of my business?"

"Okay." Lance could see that trying to brush her off wasn't working, and she didn't seem inclined to fall for vague responses. She was too intelligent and perceptive to be duped by ambiguous—or flat out, false—statements, so he told the truth. "You're the daughter, an only child, of Franklin Hathaway, and now have full control of his estate and holdings."

He noticed a shadow of grief wash over her.

"All of which I'd gladly give away to have him back," she said quietly.

Lance tried to steer the conversation in a different direction. "It's my understanding that you are intending to travel."

Her gazed darted up from where it had been staring blankly. "Yes. But it won't be the first time. I've practically grown up on the road. I think I can handle it myself."

"I have no doubt about that." Lance stopped himself from commenting further on her ability to take care of herself. "But it wouldn't hurt to have a little extra security, right? Someone thinks you need it."

Ashley let out her breath in exasperation, but Lance couldn't tell if she was annoyed at him—or the situation in general. Then he followed her gaze down to his hand, and realized he'd been absently petting the head of the dog that had come over to check him out. "Garth, come." She patted the seat beside her. When Garth hesitated, she stared at the dog curiously and somewhat grumpily. "He doesn't usually do that. He's very protective."

"I guess he knows a good man when he sees one."

She turned her head away, as if trying to ignore the sight of Lance, and tapped the fingers of her right hand on the arm of the sofa, obviously deep in thought. At last, she looked up at him. "Okay."

"Okay, what?"

"Okay. I'll let you do what it is you're supposed to do—or at least I won't stop you. But there will be rules."

Lance laughed out loud at the thought that this young woman, who probably weighed a hundred and twenty pounds fully dressed and soaking wet, was going to give *him*, Jarrod Landis, a set of rules. But then he saw the look on her face, and realized she was serious. He crossed his arms and eyed her warily. "What kind of rules?"

"You can't get in my way."

"In your way from doing what?"

She stood up and threw her hands in the air. "I don't see how this is going to work."

"Why not? You've had security before. I read that you once had twelve people in your immediate circle."

She swung around, and pointed her finger at him. "That's your first mistake."

Lance cocked his head in a questioning manner.

"Don't believe everything you read about me." She took a step toward him. "In fact, don't believe *anything* you read about me."

The look on her face was severe and steadfast. Even after what felt like a full minute, she did not remove her gaze from his.

"Okay. Deal."

She nodded and began to pace. "Rule number two."

"Wait. How many rules did you say there would be?"

"I didn't." She gave a fling of her head. "I'm making them up as I go. Rule number two," she continued as if there had been no interruption, "you're on a need-to-know basis."

"Need-to-know basis about what?"

"About me. Ask me no questions and I'll tell you no lies."

"I think I know everything I need to already." Lance did not try to hide the annoyance in his voice.

"There you go again." She threw her hands up in the air. "Judging me by what you've read. You probably expected me to be lying on a chaise lounge dressed in a sparkling evening gown."

Lance raised his brows and tilted his head to make it obvious she was right about that. How else would he evaluate her? He'd seen picture after picture, and read story after story of her temper tantrums, her wild shopping sprees, the negligent use of limos that brought traffic to a standstill. It was nothing for her to order one of her father's jets and fly to Miami for lunch with friends, then do a little shopping to the tune of tens of thousands of dollars. All of this was public knowledge—and the public seemed to love it. Her face graced the front pages of the tabloids every time the photographers could get close enough to take a shot, and the sensational stories about her knew no bounds.

After typing her name into a search engine, Lance figured he must be the only one on the planet who didn't know who she was. He began to think that was the reason Colt chose him for the job—not just because he was the NFG. No other guy worth his man card would want to get within shouting distance of a woman like this—drop-dead gorgeous, or not.

She cleared her throat as if to get his attention. "Rule number three—"

"Now wait just a minute…"

She ignored his attempt to stop her. "Rule number three. You have to sign an NDA."

Lance blinked. "A non-disclosure agreement?"

Ashley nodded. "You have a problem with that?"

"Yes, I have a problem with that," Lance exploded. "I'm a professional. I've been sent into cities and countries you've never even heard of, been told things you better hope you never hear about, and been trusted with some of this country's most sensitive secrets. Why in the hell would *I* have to sign an NDA?"

"So you don't *disclose* anything." Her voice sounded bored and impatient.

"What in the hell would I want to disclose about you—and why?"

"I don't know. It's a standard thing in showbiz." She shrugged as if she didn't understand why he was so perturbed. "It's no big deal."

Lance stared at her a moment, pondering her with an analytical gaze. "Yeah. I think I get it now."

"You get what?"

"I get *you*. You're just making up rules, thinking I'll get pissed enough to turn and walk out the door. You know this isn't the kind of job I usually do, and you don't want me around."

Her face turned a shade that was not quite red, but was certainly rosier than it had been.

"Is it working?" She looked up at him with big, blue, hopeful eyes.

"No, it's not working. I was hired to do a job, and I'm not leaving until it's done."

"Dammit." Ashley squeezed her temples as if she had a terrible headache. "You guys are all alike."

"What did you say?" Lance wasn't sure he'd heard her correctly.

"I said…never mind." She took a sip of her water, and stared into space as if she were deep in thought. "Tell you what," she said at last in a slightly less irritable tone, "let's finish this conversation in the barn. I have work to do."

Chapter 4

shley Hathaway tried to control her racing thoughts as she walked along the stone path to the barn. Garth followed on her right heel, and the sound of the solid footsteps taking up the rear indicated that the man named Lance was still here. Her heart sank. He hadn't given up yet.

"Where's all your staff?"

"What?" She turned her head, perturbed at the interruption.

"Your staff," he repeated, as he increased his stride to close the distance between them. "I thought you'd have maids and gardeners, house servants, bodyguards, cooks…"

"What would make you think that?" She tried to make it sound like she was curious and innocent—not like she was stalling with the hopes of thinking of a better answer.

She glanced at him, just for a split second, but that's all it took to see that he wasn't falling for it. The look on his face was stern. Serious. All business.

"Try again," he said.

"Umm, today's Saturday. I don't make them work weekends." She concentrated her attention on the ground, because he was now walking right beside her. Damn, he was tall. She didn't need to look at him to feel his height and his strength—and she didn't dare look up and get lost in those captivating eyes. They were dangerous. Mesmerizing. She cleared her throat in an attempt to straighten her thoughts. "There are some part-time people here that come and go."

"I'll need their names, their security background checks, and their schedules."

Ashley stopped walking. "I beg your pardon?" She raised her gaze by mistake and quickly looked away. *Dammit.* Why did he have to keep looking at her like that? Or more importantly, why did his eyes have such an effect on the rhythm of her heart? She met handsome men all the time, and was constantly propositioned by those with wealth and power. Why did this one cause a reaction that she'd never felt with the others?

She knew the answer with just another sideways glance. The men she came into contact with were mostly those who had inherited their wealth. They wore scarves and gold necklaces—and wouldn't be caught dead in a pair of wear well-worn jeans like this guy named Lance was wearing. *Thank goodness for that.* She inadvertently glanced at him again, and worked hard to suppress a sigh. They wouldn't look like *that* in them even if they did.

Ashley heard him clear his throat and knew he was waiting for a response. She shook her head to stop her roaming thoughts and concentrated instead on the conversation. "Oh, I guess you mean you need all of that information from a security standpoint."

"Yes, from a security standpoint," he repeated with an impatient tone. "How many people have the code for the entry gate?"

"You mean besides you?" she shot back without thinking. Attractive and entrancing or not, he was getting on her nerves.

He reached out and pulled her to a stop. "Look," he said, bending down and forcing her to look into his eyes again.

Ashley let out her breath slowly as she studied him and realized that she was mistaken about the intensity and color of his eyes. At first glance she'd taken them as a soft, dark brown. Now that she was standing this close—and staring straight into them—she realized they were almost as dark as his wavy black hair. Dark. Dangerous. Fascinating. Spellbinding. Her hands curled into fists as she fought the attraction and the vibrant vitality he exuded.

"I'm here to provide security. Any cooperation you provide would be greatly appreciated." His steady gaze bore into her in silent expectation.

Ashley pulled away and continued down the pathway, trying to decide what to do. Her mind wandered back to how this had all started, and zeroed in on her father's friend, Rad. She appreciated the fact that he wanted her to be safe, but it would have been nice if he'd asked for her opinion on the matter first. There were things he didn't know…things that no one knew besides her. And it would be better if it stayed that way.

This Lance guy seemed nice enough. Lord knows he was handsome enough. But she'd already come to accept that there were things she needed to do herself now that her father was gone. She wanted to protect Franklin Hathaway's reputation and legacy, and she was the only one who could do it.

"I appreciate your concern for my safety, but I'm not helpless."

She heard a snort from behind her, but continued in spite of it. "Oh, I get it. You think that because I'm rich, I can't do anything for myself." She turned around to look at him. "Strike two. I told you not to assume anything."

"Point taken. Maybe I did assume…a little. But what about security? Tell me what you have in place to protect your assets here." His tone sounded a little gentler now, as if he was at least making an attempt to be pleasant. "I saw some paintings in the house that have to be pretty expensive. I'm sure you have jewelry, furs…"

"Well, there's a security gate, *obviously*."

"Yes, but no one is manning it." He paused a moment, apparently for effect. "Or do you give the security guards the weekend off too?" He waved his hand in the air in an obnoxiously flippant manner. "Of course, everyone knows criminals don't work on Saturday and Sunday."

The tone of his voice infuriated her. She stopped right in front of him, making him come to an abrupt halt once again as well. "There are no guards because you have to have a code to get in." She titled her head and eyed him coldly. "A code. For security. So that people I don't know can't get in. Speaking of which…"

"Yes, I was given the code—probably by Uncle Rad," he said calmly. "So what happens when someone comes through the gate if no one is watching the security camera?" He straightened up and crossed his arms. "Judging from experience, I'd say *nothing*."

"I didn't say that no one was watching. They're just not on site."

"Not on sight? What does *that* mean?"

"It means they're in a security office somewhere monitoring any breaches."

He leaned down and talked in a condescending and questioning tone. "Then how would they respond to a threat?"

She shrugged and lifted her palms up. "How would I know? Call the police I guess."

She watched his expression change, and could almost read what he was thinking. She had walked into his trap, and had just proven to him the necessity of needing protection. He'd punched in the code and entered the grounds without anyone even noticing. *Chalk one up for Uncle Rad.* He knew how stubborn the daughter of Franklin Hathaway could be, and had made sure she wouldn't be able to win this argument. That's why he'd given out the code.

Ashley crossed her arms, and stared at the tree limbs overhead. She knew that the wealth she had inherited made her a target for criminals, and the fact that she was a popular public figure doubled the threat. She also knew that for men like Rad and this Lance guy, the fact that she wasn't the least bit knowledgeable—or even concerned—about her home's security, blew her risk assessment off the charts.

"Okay, the security firm is one my dad hired. I think they were friends of his and he wanted to help them get up and running with their new business." She waved her hand in the air as if all of that was inconsequential. "But that's why I have Garth here. He's all the protection I need."

"So back up a minute and let me get this straight." The tone of his voice was all business, but it implied he didn't quite believe what he was hearing. "You're here by yourself most of the time and you don't have an actual security system?"

"It's worked fine so far." She began walking again, and heard him following.

"That just means no one has tried anything yet. Anyway…" Lance reached down and patted the dog's head, who was lagging behind her. "Garth is obviously a pet. Not a watchdog."

"He's *not* just a pet. He's been professionally trained." Ashley's voice indicated her annoyance. "Believe me, he can be aggressive."

She kept moving, but smiled when she heard a low growl come from the dog. Garth had shown the ability to grasp the meaning of human conversation more times than she could count. His response indicated he'd understood what she had just said, and was verifying her assertion about his ability to be aggressive. But when she followed the direction of Garth's hostile gaze, and took in his stance and the bristled fur running the length of his back, she came to a sudden stop. Lance followed suit, but not before almost running into the back of her.

Both stood silently and stared at the sight before them. Spray-painted on the side of the barn right in front of them was a crudely drawn eyeball.

"What does that mean?" Lance looked at Ashley's face, which had turned as pale as the whitewashed barn.

"He's watching me."

Chapter 5

L ance reached for the gun under his shirt and pulled Ashley behind him with the other hand almost in a single movement. He could feel her trembling as he held onto her, but he didn't have time to worry about that right now. His eyes and his head were on a swivel, looking for anything else out of the ordinary, or any sudden movement.

"We need to get back up to the house."

"T-take the four-wheeler." Ashley nodded toward the farm vehicle parked about fifteen feet away.

"You drive." Lance didn't hesitate a moment as he pulled her toward the seat, while his gun swept back and forth, looking for hostiles. "I'll keep watch." They jumped into the farm transport, enthusiastically followed by Garth. The hair along the dog's back was still bristled and stiff, but he bounded into the back seat as if familiar with riding along.

The trip back to the house was a fast one. Lance pushed Ashley up the porch steps in front of him as he covered her from behind. When she reached the door, he pulled her to a stop so he could go through first to check for any traps or surprises. Once he entered the foyer and found it clear, he reached back and pulled her through. "Do you have a safe room?"

"No-o. But follow me." She ran up the staircase, taking two steps at a time, just as he had seen her do coming down them earlier that morning. Garth, who was no longer in watchdog mode, tore up the stairs ahead of Ashley, seeming to enjoy his position as the winner of the race up the stairs.

After leading the way down a long hallway, he stopped in front of a door on the right and wagged his tail. Lance grabbed the handle and tore the door open, swept the room with his gun, and then allowed Ashley and Garth just enough time to enter before he slammed it closed and locked it. He remained with his back against the wooden frame, staring at Ashley.

She stood in the middle of the room, bent over and breathing hard. She refused to meet his gaze, so he turned his attention to his surroundings. They had entered a bedroom that was larger than most family rooms, yet the space was devoid of the glitz and glamor that marked the rest of the house. The antique furnishings and simple decor gave it an air of elegance and charm.

Lance's gaze fell upon the tall four-poster bed on the far side of the room, and then moved to the fireplace that graced the opposite wall. The floors were bare, and appeared to be original pinewood planks, rough and scratched with age. There were no lush carpets or chandeliers; no gold-gilded frames hanging on the walls. It was if he had stepped back in time—or leaped from a world full of color to one that was black and white. It was calming. Entrancing. Soothing.

Striding to a large window on the far side of the room, he pushed aside the curtain and studied the area below.

Even though he couldn't see the barn through the trees, he measured the distance with his eyes. Then he turned toward the driveway, calculating the most direct path the intruder would have used to get onto the property and down to the barn. "Are you going to let me in on what's going on now?" His tone indicated his irritation, but he did not remove his eyes from the view out the window. Only when she remained perfectly quiet did he turn.

Ashley was now sitting in a chair near the fireplace, straight and stoic, with her hands crossed on her lap as if she were attending a formal event. She seemed to feel the intenseness of his gaze on her, and lowered her eyes down to her hands. "I don't know really."

"Maybe I should call *Uncle Rad* and ask him?"

Her head jerked up. "No. Don't do that." She stood and began to pace, her brow furrowed in deep concentration.

Lance followed her movements with nothing but his eyes. Her steps were stiff now, no longer the agile, athletic ones he'd seen before. "I'm here to help," he said, softly.

She stopped and gazed up at him. "I know...but there's a lot you don't know."

"No kidding." He crossed his arms. "I kind of figured that part out already." He waited a moment. "Why don't you fill me in?"

She flopped into the large chair again and closed her eyes. "It's complicated."

"It always is. Start at the beginning."

"All right." She opened her eyes and leaned forward. "My father was pretty well known—"

"Again, I know that much." Lance didn't even let her finish. His patience had reached its limit about an hour ago. "Jump ahead a little…to something I don't know."

"Okay. When Dad was in the process of shooting his last movie, he met a woman who asked for his help."

"Help with what?"

Ashley twisted her mouth to the side, deep in thought. "Help with a story she was working on. She wanted to expose the Hollywood culture."

"I'm not following."

She squeezed her temples. "All I know is that I accidentally picked up the phone at the same time as my father did…"

"And so you *accidentally* heard something?"

She nodded.

Lance waited as patiently as he could. She sat staring into space, and he could tell that whatever she'd heard that day really bothered her.

"I didn't recognize the voice…at first." She stopped and caught her breath. "But he told my father to stop working with Judy—"

"Back up." Lance raised his hand in the air. "Judy is the woman you just mentioned?"

She nodded.

"And you didn't recognize the voice *at first*, but you know who it is now?"

Again she nodded, but did not remove her gaze from the far wall. Her lip trembled noticeably. "Tony Sturgis."

"The big media mogul? The one who makes or breaks anyone trying to get a start in Tinsel Town?" What Lance knew about Hollywood came from reading the headlines of the tabloids while standing in line at the checkout counter. For the most part, he wouldn't be able to identify a top celebrity from a lineup. But this was one name he recognized—maybe because Sturgis was rumored to have ties to organized crime, and possibly even Mexican drug cartels. Everyone in the security business knew the name and had heard the stories, but no one had ever been able to prove anything.

She nodded.

"So this has something to do with the woman who wanted your father's help? This Judy?"

"Yes. She was working on a story as a journalist."

"So, she was writing an article." Lance continued to try to connect the dots. "On what exactly?"

"Like I said, the culture of Hollywood."

"You're going to have to explain that."

Ashley sounded exasperated, but whether it was directed toward him or the entire situation, Lance wasn't sure.

"I'm sure you've heard about the casting couch; the things that are expected in order to get a part."

"Of course, I've heard the gossip." Lance studied her while he talked. "But I always thought it was some kind of an urban legend, something that just continued to get passed around and was accepted as truth."

"Well, it's not a legend. It's true. There were crimes committed. Terrible crimes—" The breath caught in Ashley's throat. "Let's just say it's worse than anyone imagined. No one talked about it openly, but everyone knew. Everyone," she repeated.

"Until Judy…and your father." Lance bent down in front of Ashley, and spoke more gently, hoping he could get a little more information out of her that way. "So this Judy, since she's an investigative journalist, she probably knows a good bit about what's going on. I'd like to talk to her. Do you have a way to contact her?"

"No."

"If your father talked to her on the phone, I can just have someone search the records. That won't be a problem." Lance pulled out his own cell, and began to call a member of Phantom Force's team who would be able to track down the call history.

"No. You can't."

"Yes. I can." He laughed. "Believe me, we do this all the time. Piece of cake." He held the phone to his ear and put the other hand on his hip as he waited for the call to connect.

"You don't understand." Her deep blue eyes glistened. "She's dead."

Chapter 6

"Excuse me?" Lance pushed the *end call* button and slowly lowered the phone from his ear. "Did you just say what I think you said?"

"She was in the car with my father."

"Whoa." Lance wanted to reach out and comfort her, but before he could think of what to do or say, she spoke again.

"You must have heard the stories that were written." She bit her lip and paused a moment, as if trying to rein in her emotions. "That they were having an affair. That my father was drunk." She looked up at him. "The negative press was all Tony's doing. He controls everything."

"What do the police have to say about this?"

"They say it's best that I just accept that the car crash was an accident."

"Might be a good idea," Lance said. "You don't want them to know that you suspect something. There's no telling what lengths people will go to in order to keep their power."

"I know what lengths they will go to," she said quietly, staring over his shoulder.

Again, Lance felt the urge to comfort her, but wasn't sure it was his place to do so. He didn't have to make the decision. A moment later, she took a step toward him and fell into his arms sobbing. "I'm sorry. I still can't believe he's gone."

Her breath came in short gasps and her arms tightened around him.

Lance did not have much experience in comforting crying women or talking to people who were grieving. The only advice he could think of was that which had been given to him on numerous occasions in the military. *Embrace the suck.*

He successfully suppressed the urge to offer these words of encouragement, deciding they weren't quite right for this situation, and instead came up with, "It's okay." He rubbed her back and gently pushed the hair from her face when she finally looked up.

"Sorry." She took another step back. "Sometimes it just hits me and I can't stop it."

"I understand. I'm sorry for your loss."

"Almost everyone loved my dad—not just because he was rich and powerful—but because he was a good man. He was known for his integrity."

"What's the *almost* part about?"

She looked down as if choosing her words carefully. "He was loved by the fans of his movies, the actors he worked with, and most everyone he came into contact with."

"*But...*" Lance encouraged her to continue.

"But..." Ashley's brow creased as she thought about it. "He was disliked by the Hollywood establishment. He didn't follow the rules."

"Meaning?"

"Sex. Violence. His movies were tame by Hollywood standards. They didn't like that."

"They didn't like that he gave people what they wanted to see?"

She nodded. "It doesn't make sense, but it's true. He'd just had a movie released and another in production when he was killed."

"And you don't think it was just a car accident."

She shook her head violently. "No."

"So, just to be clear. This isn't just some conspiracy theory that you saw on social media—"

"No! The information he was working on with Judy hit a little too close to home for some."

"Do you know exactly what it was that they were working on?"

"Just that it was a story about the move industry and its inner workings."

"That sounds pretty innocent."

"Nothing about Hollywood is innocent. It hit some nerves."

"Why?"

"Because of what they found. Judy said she didn't set out with an agenda. She was just doing some digging around."

"And what they found *was*?" Lance pushed for more.

Ashley closed her eyes. "Sex. Money. Drugs. Organized crime."

"You're sure about that?"

"Yes." She looked up at him. "Needless to say, bringing attention to how the movie industry really works didn't earn Frank Hathaway any friends in the industry. All of the established actors, lawyers, and the top agencies stood to lose a good bit of money if movie-goers got spooked and stopped spending their money on films."

"I see. But murder? I mean it's possible, I guess. But proving it is something entirely different."

Ashley's face lost its color again. "I'm going to prove it. You can count on that."

Lance crossed his arms. "And how exactly are you going to do that?"

"I don't know yet, but I am."

Lance exhaled deeply. He could see she was passionate and determined, but he knew that would never be enough. "How much of the project was finished before...?"

Her eyes took on a faraway look. "They were still doing research. That's as far as they got. I'm still trying to track it all down."

"And how is *that* going?"

Her face lost its hopeful expression as she dropped her head. "I'll admit I've been running into some roadblocks."

"Like what?"

"People agree to help, and then suddenly change their minds."

"So you think someone is threatening them?"

"Of course."

"Maybe that means it's time to bring in some help. Someone breached this property today to send a warning to you."

Her lip trembled slightly. "They are trying to scare me."

It occurred to Lance that they were doing a good job, but his mind was busy focusing on what had occurred outside the property during his arrival that morning. He gazed at the ceiling as he remembered the fast-moving car that had caused him to veer to the shoulder of the road. No, it wasn't a car. It was a small van. The image of the man and the vehicle appeared before his eyes like a snapshot in time. Though he had only seen them for a split second, he remembered them both vividly.

"Any idea who's behind all this?" He focused his attention back on Ashley.

"The person who stands to lose the most," she said, confidently. "Tony Sturgis."

"He really has that much power?"

"He controls *everything*," she said again. "The media. Celebrities. Even politicians."

Lance made a mental note to check with some of his contacts on the background of Tony Sturgis. Despite the plentiful rumors, he wanted to know what some of the top investigators knew to be true.

"So the night he was killed, where was your father going?"

"I'm not sure, but I think to the police." Her chin quivered slightly, but otherwise she held it together. "I think he and Judy had everything they needed to bring actual charges."

"What kind of charges?"

Ashley closed her eyes. "Blackmail. Money laundering. Extortion." She cleared her throat. "Rape...Murder."

Lance let out the breath he'd been holding. He didn't know what he was expecting with this operation, but he knew it wasn't this. "So if your conspiracy theory is correct, and someone knew they were heading to the police, that means your father's phone was tapped? They knew where he was going and with whom?"

She nodded again. "Or Judy's. Or both."

"Do you think your dad had hard evidence? A computer file? Memory stick? Information printed out on paper? Anything?"

She blinked as if to wipe away any emotion, and then looked away. "My father carried his laptop with him everywhere. I know it had to be in the car that night, but the police said they never found it."

"Are you kidding me? Did you tell them all of this?"

"Of course."

"And?"

"They filed a missing property report on the computer. End of story."

Lance was beginning to see why Colt had repeatedly told him not to assume things with this case—and how badly he'd failed at that simple command. First, he'd assumed Ashley Hathaway was going to be a rich, spoiled brat. Then he'd assumed this was going to be a boring, tedious op. And lastly, he'd assumed, the next few days were going to be uninteresting and *easy.*

"Back to the conversation you overheard." Lance tried to re-focus on the missing pieces. "The person on the phone threatened your father in what way?"

"He told him to stop the investigation or he would pay with his career."

"And your father's reaction?"

Ashley's gaze met Lance's' for the first time. "He laughed. My father wasn't afraid of anyone or anything. He was respected by those he worked with. He knew he had nothing to worry about."

"I have a feeling there's a '*but*' coming."

Her eyes took on that faraway look again. "Then Sturgis mentioned me."

"In what way?"

"He just mentioned my name. That's all. But it made my father's attitude change." Her eyes welled up. "He knew what this monster could do."

She pulled away and sat on the edge of the bed with her face in her hands. "Look what happened to my father." She let her hands drop and talked as if in a trance. "Tony controls everyone and everything. He's too powerful to ever face charges."

"No one is too powerful for justice."

"You don't understand." She shook her head. "He even controls the cartels. He can have innocent people executed with a click of his fingers. Anyone who gets in his way will be destroyed one way or the other."

"Don't worry, I can deal with Tony."

"No. You don't understand what he can use against you. Politicians. The media. You don't stand a chance."

Lance wanted to know what she meant by that, but he didn't press her anymore on the subject. The look on her face was too full of pain to continue down that path. He'd pursue it some other time, when things didn't look so bleak. He decided to change the subject entirely. "What does Rad know about this?"

"Not much, I don't think." She glanced up at him with an

expression that showed relief that he hadn't kept pushing. "I think my father was pretty tight-lipped about everything he was working on, especially since he didn't want anyone else getting mixed up with the likes of Tony."

She was silent a moment, but Lance could tell her mind was active. He didn't interrupt her thoughts

"Rad probably instinctively knew something wasn't quite right," she continued, "but he didn't know the details."

She stopped talking again and bit the side of her cheek, a habit, Lance was beginning to learn, meant she had something else to say.

"And?" he prodded.

She cleared her throat. "Rad called me a few months ago and wanted me to hire additional security, to really lock this place down. He even offered to send some of the guys he works with—"

"But?"

"I couldn't let him." Her voice was hoarse and strained as she stood and began to pace. "Don't you see? If I did, then Tony would know that I know." She stopped suddenly, and looked back at him.

"Tony would know that you know *what*?"

She let out her breath in apparent exasperation that she had said more than she intended to. "That he's behind all of this. I heard him tell my father that if Dad went to the police or added additional security or told *anyone*, he would know it."

"So?"

"So, instead of *calling* the police, he and Judy were heading there in person to tell everything." She half-stifled a sob. "He killed them!"

"You don't know that."

"Yes, I do. I know Judy worked undercover...so she had proof. She had to have shown my father enough evidence to make him willing to help her—to risk his own reputation and safety."

Lance studied the view out the window again, and let out a long breath as his mind continued working. "Okay, so in other words, *that's* why there's no one around here then."

When his statement was met with silence, he glanced back at her.

"Kind of." She avoided looking at him as she talked. "I wanted everyone to think that I don't know anything—or suspect anything. That I've become a recluse since my father's death." She swallowed hard, and looked up as if determined to remain strong. "So...that's pretty much why I don't want you around, either."

"And that's pretty much why I'm staying." Lance lifted the curtain and checked for any movement outside again.

Ashley stood and threw her hands in the air. "Didn't you ever hear of the saying, *the client is always right?*"

"Yes, but that doesn't mean I believe it."

"Are you saying *you* know better than *I* do how to handle my life?"

He tilted his head ever so slightly, and raised his eyebrows, then turned back to the window without answering.

"Why you arrogant...patronizing...egotistical...*snoot.*"

"Snoot?" Lance couldn't suppress a smile as he turned back to face her. "Did you just call me a snoot?"

She crossed her arms and looked away.

"Congratulations," he said.

"Congratulations on what?" she snipped.

"I've been called a lot of things in my life—but never a snoot. You're the first."

"Ha. Ha. Glad you think it's so funny."

"I'm not sure if it's funny or not, to tell you the truth. In fact, I'm not even sure I know what a snoot is."

"*None* of this is funny. You broke through my security gate this morning, walked into my house, and now you're standing here in my bedroom, acting like I hired you to do something."

"Fact check number one: I didn't break through your gate." Lance moved in close to her. "I had the code. Fact check number two: I didn't just walk into your house, the guy named Stan let me in. And fact check number three: I'm standing in your bedroom because someone sent you a threatening message. They were able to do so, I might add, by gaining access through a gate that is supposedly secure."

"So? What business is that of yours?"

Lance opened his eyes wide and stared at her like he thought perhaps she was kidding. "Hello? I'm here to *protect* you."

"From what?"

"Yourself, apparently," he mumbled under his breath.

"What did you say?"

"I said…never mind."

She gave him a look of disdain that made her blue eyes appear even more alluring. "Look. I don't see what you don't understand. If Sturgis thinks I've hired security, he'll be even more aggressive. He'll get suspicious. Who knows what he'll do? I don't want anyone to get hurt."

"As long as I am here, no one will get hurt. That's what I do," he said confidently. "Protect people."

"But you don't—"

Lance walked up to her and put his hands on her shoulders. She seemed so small and fragile all of a sudden. "Listen. No one needs to know that I'm security. I do this for a living. I can stay under the radar."

"But I have public appearances," she shot back. "Obviously they're going to *see* you."

"There's an easy way around that." His tone was all business.

"Which is?" She tilted her head and looked bewildered.

Lance held his arms out, palms up. "Meet your new boyfriend."

Chapter 7

I t took a moment for what he'd said to sink in, but once it did, Ashley was quick to react. *"That* would be a definite *no."*

"Before you overreact, think about it for a minute. It actually makes perfect sense."

"N. O." She spelled the word as if that would help him understand it. "Nooo."

"Okay, let me put it this way. You don't have a choice. You can play along, or you can make it obvious that I'm your protective service. If I'm going to be able to help you, I suggest you play along." He paused, but only for a moment, as if that's all it took for him to analyze the situation and continue to figure out what to do next. "Have you received any other communication, besides what's out there on the barn?"

He paced broodingly as he asked the question, but when she didn't answer, he stopped. His brows creased as he stared at her steadily. "I'll rephrase the question. *What kind* of communication have you received?

Ashley looked up at him, unnerved that he could figure out she was hiding something when he'd only just met her. Without thinking, she put her hand to her racing heart as if that would somehow calm it down, as Lance studied her intently.

What had started out a normal day had somehow turned into an upside down nightmare. Here she was standing with a stranger in her bedroom—a stranger that left her wobbly and out-of-breath. Confused and muddled. She tried to concentrate. Tried to focus as she stared back at the man.

At least they hadn't sent a bald, overweight rent-a-cop to help with security, she acknowledged to herself. Lance was not hard to look at, and seemed to be very good at his business. He'd removed his blazer and now wore a black collared shirt that fit snugly enough that she could see the contour of his muscles along his shoulders and ribcage. His jeans were well-worn, but appeared clean and wrinkle-free. Her gaze lifted still higher, to his hair. It was thick and wavy, the kind of hair that made women wonder what it would be like to run their fingers through it.

He crossed his arms and cleared his throat, jolting her from her musings.

"Do you ever just give up and go away?" she said, irritably.

"Don't change the subject. Answer the question." He stood in the middle of the room with his hands on his hips now, looking big and strong, and completely in control. Ashley felt like the walls of her room had shrunk tenfold. A space that had once appeared large and spacious to her seemed suddenly undersized and confining. The raw masculinity he exuded was enough to smother her.

She walked over to the bed and flopped down. "Nothing directly...but there have been signs."

"You'll need to elaborate a little on that."

"The staff has left. Not all at once. Just one by one, over the past year."

"What reason did they give?"

"At first I thought they had gotten really good job offers somewhere else."

"But?"

"But then it became obvious they were being threatened."

"Okay, what else?"

She closed her eyes as she thought about it. "Back when I was still in the public eye, people I didn't know would come up to me and say things—just in passing—but it was like they knew where I was going to be next."

"How do you think anyone would do that?"

"I don't know."

"Is your schedule publicized somewhere? A website? Social media?"

"I suppose the hosting venue might have publicized it sometimes, but I never did."

"So that's why you stopped going anywhere at all." Lance connected the dots again.

Ashley nodded and looked away. She had to. He projected an energy and power that undeniably attracted her—much as she didn't want to admit it. "I haven't been to a public event in more than ten months.

"Have you talked to the police about—"

"No!" Ashley responded before he'd even finished the sentence. "It would just bring more publicity. I don't need that right now."

"How would going to the police bring you publicity?"

"I just told you. Tony has snitches there. If he knows I'm talking to the police, he'll do something like leak a fake story to the media. My name will be all over the tabloids within hours." She glanced back at him. "Anyway, isn't that why you're here?"

"It's kind of hard to provide security when I don't know what's going on."

"I've just told you everything. I don't know what else could possibly help you."

Lance put one hand to his temples and squeezed. "Well, to tell you the truth, a couple of things aren't adding up to me."

"Such as?" She gazed up questioningly, her blue eyes wide and inquisitive.

"What's up with the stories I've seen? The extravagant spending? Lavish trips? I'll admit I only met you a little over an hour ago, but it doesn't seem to fit."

Ashley stared at him unblinking as the clock on the mantle ticked off the seconds. "What are you, some kind of perceptive clairvoyant psychic robocop?"

"No. But I know a spoiled, overindulged, bad-tempered female when I see one."

"Meaning?"

"I saw one in the videos and media stories I reviewed." He paused a moment. "I'm not looking at one now."

She stood and began to pace, this time chewing on one of her nails.

"You may as well level with me," Lance said. "I'm going to get to the bottom of this one way or the other."

"Damn you, Rad," she muttered, before stopping in the

middle of the floor, and eyeing him from over her shoulder. "Can I request someone else from your company? I'll tell your boss we just don't mesh."

Lance shrugged. "Probably. But none of the other guys are nearly as patient as I've been or half as tolerant." He didn't smile. He wasn't kidding. "At least one of them would have thrown you over his lap and spanked you by now."

"If that's a joke, it isn't funny."

Lance didn't bother to respond. He just tilted his head to the side, and glared at her in such a way that she got the message he was serious. "Either level with me, or I'm going to call my boss and tell him you've requested Shank. Then, we'll see if I'm joking."

Ashley blinked her eyes repeatedly, as if she were envisioning what the guy named Shank would look like.

"Okay. Okay. No need to get other people involved in this." She took a deep breath. "It sounds crazy now, but it was a game, really."

"A game?"

She exhaled, showing her frustration—and embarrassment. "What you saw were the years when I was twenty or twenty-one. I was young, immature, so it was fun pretending to be a spoiled brat. I only did it as a way to help my father."

"So it was a publicity stunt?"

"If you look at the timing, it was always right before a premier of one of my father's movies."

"So-o-o, the paparazzi followed you around, gave you headlines, provided sound bites—"

"And I would mention my father's movie. Boom." She

clapped her hands together. "Free promotion."

Lance nodded thoughtfully as he stared at the young, serious woman, who was nothing like he had envisioned or expected. She was mature. Smart. Independent. Quiet.

"Dad didn't like it…" She paused and took a deep breath. "But he always let me learn lessons the hard way."

"And the lessons you learned?"

She didn't hesitate. "It's not really that fun pretending to be someone you're not." She closed her eyes. "And a good reputation is easier to keep than regain."

Lance stared at her thoughtfully. "Your father must have been quite a man. I'm sorry I never got to meet him."

Her eyes opened and glistened unnaturally. "Yes, he was."

The room grew quiet for a moment, but Ashley could tell that Lance was only trying to figure out how to broach the subject he'd thus far avoided. She knew it was a topic that he wouldn't avoid, no matter how embarrassing it was for her.

As expected, he took a deep breath and plunged right in. "I'm curious about the other stories—"

She turned around abruptly, before he could even finish. "If you're talking about so-called drug use, *that* was Tony."

Lance raised his eyebrows questioningly. "Go on."

"I told you he controlled the media…or at least they were happy to print whatever he told them to print. He wanted to make sure I knew he meant business, so he leaked a story that I'd been arrested at the airport with cocaine, and that I'd paid the authorities to keep it quiet." She looked him straight in the eyes. "It never happened."

"I see." Lance rubbed his chin as he absorbed the new

information. "So the original story was front-page news, and the correction—if there was one—was played down."

She didn't respond with anything other than a slight nod of her head, but Lance must have seen how much the experience had hurt her by the expression she wore. He changed the subject.

"Let's figure out where we need to start. What employees are left? Who can get in and out of the gate?"

"Well, Stan, of course."

"The guy I met downstairs?"

She nodded. "He was my father's right-hand man. His best friend, really."

"You trust him?"

"Absolutely." She nodded. "He loved my father. He wouldn't leave no matter how much they threatened him."

"Who else? A cook? Housecleaner?"

"Stan does all of that now."

"What about the barn? The grounds?"

"I do the barn work. We only have two horses now."

Lance nodded thoughtfully. "Okay. I'm going to go out on a limb and assume there's no one watching or checking the security footage."

Ashley's eyes darted away, and then she closed them, and exhaled deeply. "That part of the security system went bonkers a few months ago."

"Bonkers?"

"It doesn't work."

"And no one came to fix it?"

She shrugged. "Not yet."

Lance put his hand to his temples and squeezed. "Okay. So do you think one of your former staff could have given out the gate code?"

"Rad changed the code last month, just in case."

"Well, that's a good start." He started toward the door. "I still need to go have a look around. Lock the door behind me and sit tight. Okay?"

"No. I want to go along."

Lance stopped with his hand on the door, causing Ashley's gaze to drift to his left hand. No ring. And no wonder. What kind of woman would want to marry a man whose occupation involved traveling all over the world and risking his life in dangerous operations?

He started to turn around, but her mind kept wandering. No, if she had a man like Lance, she wouldn't want to let him out of her sight. She shook her head at where her thoughts were taking her. What in the hell was she doing? This guy had walked into her life, and was now standing in her bedroom, ordering her around like she was a child. Half of her didn't even like the man. The other half...well, the other half wanted him to provide more than just security.

"What did you say?"

"I said, I want to go along. I know every inch of this property. Maybe I can be of help."

As his eyes swept across her skeptically, her thoughts drifted to the long, tedious dinner parties and charity events she had attended over the years. She'd spent her entire life around men who sipped exotic drinks from crystal glasses with one pinky in the air, and looked down on anyone who didn't.

Some of them were handsome, of course. Most of them were rich. Yet somehow, she could not picture herself living with a man who spent more time in front of a mirror, and more money on skin products than she did. Her eyes locked on his, but she was still deep in thought. This one? This one was the exact opposite. This Lance guy exuded danger, strength—and sensuality—all at the same time.

The elites in Hollywood would probably look down on the raw masculinity that this man radiated. She smiled. Yes, they would even go so far as to call it toxic.

Her heart thumped violently as if to get her attention. If this was *toxic masculinity*, she wanted to drown in it.

Chapter 8

L ance kept his eyes on the ground as they walked back outside. He didn't like the idea of Ashley tagging along, but he could tell—even from the short time he had known her—that it would be easier to allow it than try to stop her. The idea of handcuffing her to a chair had entered his mind, but he decided to keep that option open for later if necessary. He forced the smile from his face at the thought of it.

As for the vehicle he'd passed on the way in this morning, Lance had already shot Colt a text to see what he could do with satellite imagery. He wanted to know everyone who went in and out of this property over the past three months.

"What vehicles have been back here?" He pointed to the tracks that went beyond where his own vehicle sat parked at the house.

"None that I know of."

"No delivery trucks? Barn workers?"

"No." Ashley shook her head, before another thought popped into her head. "Oh, except for the flower delivery, of course."

"Flowers?"

"In the house. My father had flowers delivered every day

in honor of my mother." She paused. "He loved doing it so much. I continued the tradition."

Lance stared thoughtfully at the house, as he remembered the overflowing flowers in the foyer. "The same company and the same driver?"

"Same company. I'm not sure about the driver."

"So the flower company has the code to the gate and they come in and out of here every day, right?" Lance stood with his hands on his hips. "No one really notices them because it's a regular occurrence."

"They've been delivered as long as I can remember," she said. "For the record, I don't think I have to worry about a flower guy."

"Which is why you should have security," Lance responded under his breath. Then he became all business again. "It shouldn't be too hard to get this place locked up tight. You're not still planning on traveling. Right?"

Ashley looked at him as if he were joking. "You mean other than the premier of my father's movie?"

"Is it *that* important?"

"It's my *father's* movie. He died when it was in post-production. Do you live under a rock?"

Lance ignored the jab. He might as well live under a rock for all he knew about what was happening in the alternative universe called Hollywood. Now he knew why Colt had sent him and why it was so urgent.

"When?"

"I leave Friday."

"That's the day after tomorrow."

"Impressive that you would know that."

Lance again pretended not to notice the sarcasm. "So, it looks like I have a lot of work to do in a short amount of time."

Ashley walked up to within inches of him and blinked her eyes playfully. "The only thing you really have to do is go back to wherever you came from."

"I can't do that. We've been over this. I was sent to do a job and I'm going to do it." He stared out over her shoulder as he talked, his mind already detailing all of the necessary steps he would have to take.

"If you were serious about your earlier proposal, then I think we need to talk about this a little more," Ashley said.

"What more is there to talk about?"

"I want to make sure you understand that I don't want to be seen in public with a security detail—or even a body guard. My father didn't do it that way, and neither am I."

"And I want *you* to understand that if you're doing a public appearance, you need protection. And if you don't want obvious security, then we'll have to go as a couple."

Ashley had been walking ahead. She turned in one movement. "I seriously thought you were kidding about that."

Lance held his hands up, palms out, in a gesture of innocence. "You're the one who doesn't want to be seen with security. If you want to play it that way, then that's how we'll have to do it."

She surprised him by putting her head back and laughing. Then she turned serious and scanned his body from head to toe with a swoop of her eyes. "When was the last time you wore a tux? Do you even *own* one?"

Lance stopped laughing and his lips compressed together. She had him there. He'd rented one for his brother's wedding, but that had been more than five years ago. His hesitation lasted only a moment. He had Colt backing him up. Men in the field ran into more complex and seemingly impossible tasks than this one. A simple phone call to Colt, and a tux would be forthcoming, correct size and all.

"That won't be a problem," he said. "Do you own a suitable gown?" He allowed his gaze to run up and down her body just as she had done to him. The way she was dressed at the moment, she would be more apt to be confused with a stable hand than an heiress.

Of course, prior to her father's death, she had attended premiers and dinner parties, and mingled with the rich and famous from all over the world. Still, she'd not been seen in public for almost a year.

"Is that supposed to be some kind of a joke?"

"No."

"I think I can find something," she said with a flip of her head.

"Good. When do we leave?" Lance became all business again. "I'd like to have an itinerary of your schedule, especially the parts that involve social events and interaction with the public."

She studied him with slit-eyed intensity. "I don't remember actually *accepting* your invitation."

"I don't remember actually *sending* an invitation, so what's your point?"

"My point is that your little scheme cannot possibly work."

He studied her intently, and began nodding his head. "Yep. I think you're scared."

Her head jerked toward him. "Scared? Scared of what?"

"Me." He took a step closer and bent down a little. "Don't worry. I don't bite." He waited for her to gaze to meet his. "Well, not much anyway."

Her face turned red. "I'm not afraid of you. I don't want the publicity this will bring. Where am I going to say I met you? Who am I going to say you are?"

"Oh, we'll work all that out," he responded with a wave of his hand. After taking a few moments to think about it, he snapped his fingers. "I've got it. Tell them, I'm your plumber and it was love at first sight."

"No. No. No." Her voice was no longer high and shrill like it had been before. It was low and full of anger.

"Don't go getting all temperamental on me," Lance said with a grin. "You'll ruin the impression I was beginning to get of you."

She turned her back with a huff and crossed her arms, and began talking as if to herself. "Maybe if I call Uncle Rad, I can get him to call this whole thing off."

"Don't count on it."

She whirled around. "Why not?"

"Because I've already filed a preliminary report with my boss, who is a very efficient man, and has no doubt already conversed with Rad. There's no way either one of them is going to let you go to that premier alone after what just happened at the barn." When she did not respond with anything more than a pout, he added. "Sorry to burst your bubble."

"No you're not. You're enjoying this."

"Okay. Maybe I am." He smiled and spoke softer now. "But I can assure you I'm not going to enjoy getting into a monkey suit and pretending to be somebody I'm not."

"It's easy," she said with a shrug and a faraway look. "I used to do it all the time."

Chapter 9

L ance sat in the limo on the way to the airport trying to steal a glance at the woman beside him. She was mad, he could tell, yet that seemed to only make her more attractive. She was dressed casually, yet stunningly, in a pair of tight designer jeans and slouchy leather boots. A light sweater lay draped across her shoulders and dark sunglasses covered her eyes. Sitting between them was an oversized purse made of soft, supple leather—an accessory that probably cost more than what he made in a month.

Staring down at his laptop, Lance tried to concentrate on the mission rather than the soft scent of her perfume, or the fact that she was so angry with him she wasn't talking. He read through his emails, updated Colt on his schedule, and then scanned through a news feed. When he looked up again, they were pulling onto the main road to the airport. The limo didn't stop for traffic, but bypassed a line of cars by turning down a side road to a secluded section of the runway. A gleaming private jet sat alone, waiting to depart.

"There's our ride." Ashley opened the door and jumped out, not waiting for the limo driver to come around to assist her.

Lance scooped up some loose paperwork and his computer

and jumped out the other side, trying to catch up. The steps to the aircraft were steep, but when he tried to take Ashley's arm to help her, she shrugged him off. "Good grief. I can do it."

"Just trying to help," he mumbled, as she moved in front of him while climbing the steps. The action put the sight of her tight-fitting jeans directly at his eye level, causing him to almost miss one of the steps himself.

"Welcome aboard."

Lance shook the hand of the captain as he greeted them at the bulkhead. He wanted to stop and talk, but Ashley seemed to be in a hurry, so he followed her into the plane. With his eyes roaming, he tried not to gawk. He'd been in private jets before—many of them. But none were quite as luxurious or opulent as this one. Deep-seated leather chairs stood out in contrast to wood paneled walls. On one side was a curved sofa, and on the opposite wall a large-screen television set.

Ashley glanced around and said simply. "My father traveled a good bit, and liked to do it in style."

"I see that."

She walked passed the couch and threw her purse onto a small table, before sinking into a deep fawn-colored leather chair by the window. Lance chose one of two double seats that faced each other on the other side of the aisle, and placed his laptop and papers down on the marble tabletop in front of him.

"There's a bedroom in the back if you want to lie down," she said. "And a bathroom right there." She nodded toward a door on the right.

"No thanks." Lance reclined into the soft chair. "I'm going

to get some work done."

"Suit yourself."

Lance could barely make out the mumbled words as she turned back around and opened a book. She'd made it clear she would put up with him on this trip, but would not go so far as to pretend to enjoy it.

***

Ashley tried to concentrate on the book on her lap, but she could feel Lance's eyes on the back of her head. Or was that just her imagination? Or was that what she was *hoping*? She sighed. No. Knowing Lance, he was probably already deeply engrossed in his work, not even noticing she was there. Or even *more* likely, he was playing solitaire on his computer, trying to ignore her. She let out another long sigh of exasperation at her scattered and useless thoughts.

"You okay?"

She turned around. His brown eyes appeared soft as he gazed over the top of his computer at her.

"Oh, yeah. Just umm…" She held up the book. "Just got to a good part."

He raised his eyebrows as if he didn't quite believe her, but shrugged and bent back over his work.

Ashley returned to her reading position, with her face feeling like it was on fire. *Dammit. Why does he affect me like this?*

His detached, unemotional tone and actions infuriated her. Did nothing excite him? Make him nervous? Get him scared? He was like a robot on autopilot, ready to step in at a moment's notice and take control of any situation at any given time.

Then again, he could be all business and brazen one minute, and then turn around and be kind and concerned the next. His brown eyes sometimes burned black with impatience and intolerance, but could soften to a glow full of warmth and humor, causing her heart to throb with emotion.

Maybe that's what she found so strangely infatuating about him. Ashley put her face in her hands and shook her head, causing the book to fall into her lap. *Damn him.*

"Really good chapter, huh?"

Ashley bit her lip, straightened back up and nodded, but didn't turn around. "Yeah. Really good." She forced herself to stare at the pages, even though she had no idea what was on them. With all the traveling she'd done with her father, Ashley thought that she'd met every type of human being out there. And she thought she knew how to handle herself around them pretty well too. Everyone always commented on her poise and her charm.

But this one threw her for a loop; knocked her completely off balance. She felt awkward and shy around him, like a teenage girl with a crush. *Good grief, what would Dad think if he saw me acting like this?*

That thought actually brought a smile to her face. He would like Lance. She knew he would. Her father had always worried about her finding the "right guy." He'd often told her that the guys she met in the movie industry weren't good enough. There were better men out there.

He was right, as always. Most of the men she'd been around were in show business or a related field. They weren't what you might call…well, manly. Sure, some of them were good-looking. A few of them were even ripped—if you liked the musclebound, gym-membership look. But pretty much all of them were needy, egotistical, and off-the-charts narcissistic.

Of course, being the daughter of one of the most successful movie directors of all time made Ashley very popular—and a prime target for every eligible bachelor in Hollywood. She had no illusions about the invitations she received or the number of men who pursued her. One had only to talk to them for a few seconds to know that in *their* minds, the world revolved around them. They did not flirt with her because they were interested in Ashley Hathaway. They flirted because they were interested in the daughter of Franklin Hathaway.

Lance was different, she mused. He didn't flirt—far from it. And he certainly didn't pour on the charm. At times, she questioned if he even possessed any. No. His entire demeanor and attitude were different. He confused her. Knocked her off balance. She was completely baffled as to how to handle him.

She decided on a very direct, very detached, business approach. He wasn't like the other men she'd met, so the standard rules of interaction did not apply.

Ashley hesitantly glanced over her shoulder. No. There would be no ordinary rules here. Lance was anything but average or typical. He certainly wasn't sociable and he definitely didn't flirt. In fact, he seemed perfectly content not talking at all. Or maybe he just didn't like talking to *her.* She chewed on one of her manicured fingernails. Okay, maybe he was really quite affectionate and genial when not on duty, but he was a professional and didn't like mixing business with pleasure.

One thing was for sure. He didn't come across as particularly aware of his own physique—which seemed odd to her, since it was so damned impossible to miss or ignore.

She stifled another sigh as her mind wandered to what it would be like if he wasn't so honorable and *would* mix business with pleasure. That contemplation caused her heart to throb and her thoughts to drift back to her father. Yes Lance would be his kind of guy. She could picture the two of them sitting in her father's office, drinking whiskey and smoking cigars. That was the type of son-in-law her father had always envisioned.

Wait. *Son-in-law?* Was she going flipping crazy? This time she successfully suppressed any outward show of emotion, but she did close her eyes and bite her lip again. *Stop it, Ashley. Just stop.*

***

Deep into his work, Lance was surprised when a member of the crew came back to inform him they were descending and would land in about thirty minutes, depending on other air traffic. As soon as the man exited, Ashley plopped down in the seat on the other side of the table.

"We need to talk."

"About what, *honey?*" Lance shot her a smile, hoping she would take his joke in stride.

"Stop it."

He leaned back and crossed his arms. "Okay. Sorry. What's up?"

"That's exactly the kind of thing I *don't* want happening." She leaned forward, and stared at him with her big blue eyes.

"Look, *you're* the one who doesn't want to be seen with

security in public, so basically this whole thing is *your* idea. I certainly don't do most of my ops pretending to be someone's fiancé. Just saying."

"Wait a minute. I beg your pardon." She raised both hands in the air, and cocked her head to the side. "When did we get engaged? I thought you said *boyfriend*, not *fiancé*."

"Oh, didn't I tell you?" He sat back, enjoying the sparks of emotion in her eyes. "I thought we might as well kick it up a notch. Go big or go home. Right? No sense in dragging this thing out."

Ashley appeared off balance and out of breath. "I've known you for three freaking days."

Lance leaned back in the deep leather chair and crossed his arms. "Really?" he said, with a frown. "Seems like a *lot* longer."

He could see her face turning red, but whether it was from anger at his insinuation or embarrassment, he couldn't be sure. The look lasted only a few seconds. Her attitude soon changed. "Okay then, Mr. Go-Big-Or-Go-Home. If we're engaged, where's my ring?"

"What?" He knew instantly what she meant, but he was always amazed at how quick she was with a comeback, even after being knocked off-guard.

"My ring." She held up her left hand.

Her nails were long, and painted a beautiful shade of pink that matched her lips. Lance lost his train of thought and stared. How did women do that? What kind of magic did they perform to match their nail color with the exact hue of their lips?

"Hello? R-I-N-G." She interrupted his thoughts. "You can't expect *me*, Ashley Hathaway, to be engaged, and not have a spectacular diamond ring."

Lance frowned. "You've got me there. I'm new at this marriage thing."

"Great future husband you'll be." She let out her breath in exasperation, and once again, he couldn't tell if it was aimed at him or herself. She rested her head in her hands a moment. "Okay. Maybe you're right."

"Excuse me?"

She lowered her arms and studied him. "Maybe we should pretend to be serious, so that nobody thinks it's just an act."

He leaned back and smiled. "Say it again."

"I beg your pardon?" Her brow creased. "Say what again?"

"Say, *'you're right.'* I like the sound of it."

She hit the table with both hands. "You are the most exasperating, irritating, aggravating, infuriating—"

"Whoa, baby. Sorry. Just kidding."

Ashley crossed her arms and turned her head away while rolling her eyes. Lance wasn't sure if that meant she accepted his apology or not. He had a lot to learn about this woman—and, so far, he was enjoying the education.

The idea of being her fiancé caused a sensation that was both pleasing and terrifying. He'd never allowed himself to get close to anyone before. The career he'd chosen didn't leave much room for a home life or time for a companion. The traveling, the danger, the secrets, didn't exactly lend themselves to close relationships. Heck, he didn't even own a dog.

But this woman was different. He liked her boldness and

her driving intelligence—two things he hadn't expected when he'd accepted the mission.

Glancing up at the lull in conversation, he realized she was studying him, as if trying to figure out what he was thinking. "Okay. Hard to admit, but *you're* right too…about the ring, I mean."

Her eyebrows raised in a questioning way, as if surprised that he'd admit that she was right. "That probably won't be a problem." Her voice was lighter now. "Dad has a safe here in the plane with some of mom's jewelry. I'm sure I can find something in there."

"Then we're all set."

"Except." She looked at him with her brows knitted close together. "You *are* planning to shave before we land, right?"

Lance lifted his hand to his face and rubbed his cheek. He'd worked late into the night, and they'd left early this morning. "If you want me to."

"Even if I liked the rugged, scruffy look—which I'm not saying I do…" Ashley paused a moment as if to catch her breath, and the look in her eyes indicated to Lance that she liked it very much. "It will make you stick out in this town. Men don't have beards like that."

"Why not? Can't they grow them?"

She ignored his retort, and nodded toward the back of the plane. "The bathroom is fully stocked with everything you'll need." She pulled out her phone. "We land in twenty minutes."

"That sounded distinctly like an order." Lance closed his laptop and stood. "You're getting a little controlling, aren't you, dear?"

She looked so cute with her face blossoming with color that Lance couldn't resist another jab. He turned and headed toward the restroom, but talked over his shoulder. "By the way, next time you're pretending to read a book, you should try turning the pages."

When he glanced back, Ashley sat with her arms crossed, staring straight ahead. She didn't say anything, but her expression spoke volumes.

Chapter 10

"So you have the story straight, right?" Lance glanced over at Ashley, who was applying a new layer of lipstick.

She smacked her lips together. "I think so."

"Look, we've been over this a hundred times. My name is Jack Davies, son of John Davies, an acquaintance of your father's. We met a long time ago, and then ran into each other at an event just before your father died. We've been inseparable ever since."

"Which is why I've been a recluse for the last year." Ashley let out her breath in exasperation. "But you don't understand the press. They're going to want every tidbit, every little speck of intrigue they can find. The idea that Ashley Hathaway has a fiancé is big news."

"It is?" Lance sat up a little straighter and adjusted his coat. "So I'm a pretty important guy all of a sudden? I might be able to get used to this."

"Not funny."

Lance's smile faded instantly. "I know it's not funny, but I'm trying to get you to relax a little."

"I'll relax when this is over. Let's see if you think it's such a big joke when they start making things up about you." She turned her head to stare idly through the window of the limo, her hair streaked with hints of gold. "That's how it works, you know. If they don't get it from a real source, they'll just make it up."

"Or get it from Tony?"

He saw a flash of fear in her eyes when she glanced back at him. She didn't answer, but nodded.

He reached over and patted her arm. "It will be over before you know it."

An awkward silence ensued, until Lance cleared his throat. "Do you mind if I ask a personal question?"

She shot him a questioning look. "Depends how personal it is."

"How'd you get your hair to grow so fast?"

"Excuse me?"

"Your hair. It was a lot shorter yesterday."

She tilted her head. "You're kidding, right?"

"No." He looked offended. "Just curious. If it's a secret that only women are allowed to know or something, then forget it."

"You don't get out much do you?"

"What do you mean?"

"It's called hair extensions." She ran her hand through the long locks. "Everyone uses them."

"How would I know that? This isn't exactly my world." He swept his hand toward the window.

"Yeah. Okay. Except they've only been around for about a gazillion years. I stayed up most of the night trying to get them to look right." She turned more fully toward him. "*Do* they look right?"

Lance looked at her again as if seeing her for the first time today. She wore eyeliner and mascara, and her lips were a soft glossy pink. He contrasted her to the woman he'd met a few days ago, and wasn't sure which one he liked better. This one was decidedly more feminine. Soft. Sexy.

But the other one was more natural. Genuine. Untamed.

He lifted his hand to pick a lock of hair off her shoulder. "It looks real to me."

She leaned back against the seat. "I guess that's as good of a compliment as I'm going to get from you. You could have said it looks great. Or spectacular. Or stunning. But no-o-o. You said it looks *real*."

Lance was dumbfounded. He understood from her tone that he'd said or done something wrong, but he wasn't exactly sure what it was.

"What do you think about this?" Ashley held up her hand to show off the ring.

"It looks *great*." Lance prided himself on being a fast learner.

"Of course you would say that *now*." She snorted in exasperation. "Since it's a ring you picked out for me."

"But I've never seen that ring before in my life."

She turned more fully toward him, and spoke in a low, even voice. "It's our engagement ring."

"Oh yeah," he said, realizing his mistake. "Now I remember." He paused a moment. "Where did I get it? Is that important? Is it a designer thing?"

"No, it's an heirloom actually. If anyone asks, tell them you saw it at an estate auction and knew it was perfect for me. You may not get out much..." She held up her hand and moved it back and forth to make the diamond sparkle. "But at least you have good taste in diamonds."

Lance studied the massive ring and the intricate setting. "Cost me a fortune, but you're worth it." Their gazes met over the top of the ring. If he'd expected his comment to illicit a smile, he was sadly mistaken.

"Just so we understand each other...even though we're engaged...there will be no PDA's. Okay?"

"You can't keep adding rules—"

"No PDA's. Understand?"

He leaned in close and stared into her eyes. "Do I look like the type of guy who likes to have public displays of affection?"

She looked away, as if unwilling to meet his gaze. "I don't know. Do you have a wife? A girlfriend?"

"No." He held up his right hand. "I'm not that kind of guy. You're my one and only. Scout's honor."

She grabbed his hand and pushed it down. "This isn't going to work. You would need at least a month of obedience training to get to the point of being acceptable in public."

"I might be a little anti-social, but I'm not a dog, and I don't need obedience training." Lance put his hand on hers to calm her. "I'm a professional. This is a job. I'll do what I'm told and behave in public."

She studied his eyes as if testing his sincerity, and then lowered her gaze just as a look of uncertainty crept into her expression.

"Now what's wrong?"

"What do you mean?" Her long lashes lifted, exposing the full brilliance of her eyes more fully.

"You looked like you wanted to tell me something."

She frowned as if irritated that he'd correctly interpreted her expression. "Just don't be too surprised when you see the public me. That's all."

Lance gazed at her questioningly, but the limo was slowing down and pulling up to the curb.

Chapter 11

There was no more time for conversation, but Lance had no problem sensing the irritation that radiated from Ashley's tense posture. When the vehicle finally came to a stop, Lance reached for the door handle, but she grabbed his arm. "Let the chauffeur open it." She shot him a nervous smile. "And if you don't want your face all over the tabloids, keep your hat on and your head down."

He nodded, remembering that he wasn't supposed to be in the security business. He was a bridegroom, engaged to one of the wealthiest—and most beautiful—women in the country.

"And try not to look so damn masculine," she whispered as her door opened and a white-gloved hand was extended to help her out of the car.

Lance just smiled and waited for her to depart, before sliding across the seat and out the same door. When he stood and reached for her arm, the click and flash of a few dozen cameras from the media almost caused him to throw her back into the car. Instead, he put his chin down, so that only the top of his hat and the bottom of his chin were visible.

"Miss Hathaway." A nervous-looking man wearing a big smile stepped forward from the crowd and took her hand. "Such a pleasure to have you staying with us." He glanced over at Lance. "And I see you've brought a friend.

"Mr. Jenkins. It's so nice to see you again." Ashley allowed him to kiss her on each cheek, before turning to Lance. "Yes, this is…"

"Jack Davies." Lance stepped forward with his right hand extended when Ashley faltered. "A pleasure to meet you. Ashley has told me many wonderful things about your hotel."

He felt, rather than saw, Ashley give him a sideways glance, but the complement sent the hotel manager into a new round of conversation. "Oh we love having Miss Hathaway as a guest. That we do," he said. "I'll have your bags sent up. Please let me know if there is anything I can do for you."

Lance continued to keep his head down as he led Ashley past a few more photographers that had positioned themselves inside the hotel. A bellman stood holding the elevator for them, and when the door closed, both Ashley and Lance exhaled, as if they'd just run through a gauntlet.

When the elevator dinged for their floor, the bellman motioned for them to follow. "I know my way. Thank you." Ashley started to hand the man a tip, but Lance intervened, and slid the man a twenty. "Thank you. I hope you enjoy your stay." The bellman gave Lance a curious look and then stepped back into the elevator.

"Let me go in first." Lance turned the knob and slowly pushed open the door, before stepping inside. The view that greeted him was unlike anything he'd ever seen before. The entryway of black marble was graced by a small table with a vase overflowing with fresh flowers. A full-length gold-plated mirror reflected the glistening prisms from the chandelier hanging from the twelve-foot ceiling.

He continued into the penthouse, his eyes looking left and right as he descended down three polished marble stairs into the living room that was bigger than most houses. Two white pillars flanked the room on one side, and sunlight streamed in from a wall of windows on the other.

The mosaic pattern of the floor was highlighted by a large dark blue rug, accented with gold. Two white couches faced one another, and four other chairs were arranged around a gas fireplace.

Ashley pushed past him and continued into the room. "No one else can get onto this floor without a card," she said. "I think it's safe."

She pulled the sweater off her shoulders as she walked. "I've been counting the minutes to get these off." Flopping onto one of the plush sofas, she kicked off the leather boots.

Lance continued checking out the space, which more closely resembled a luxurious house than a hotel room. There was a dining room with a table for eight, a spacious living room with a breathtaking view, two large bedrooms, and three bathrooms. A wraparound furnished terrace offered views toward Hollywood Hills.

The two bedrooms were located at opposite ends of the suite, and both featured a lounge area, walk-in closet, and a full bathroom with whirlpool tub and oversized shower.

He came back to where she was sitting. "I don't think this is going to work."

She looked up at him and laughed. "Not good enough for your taste?" When she saw he was serious, her smile disappeared. "Why not?"

"The bedrooms." He nodded toward the open doorway where a king-sized bed was in view. "They're on opposite sides."

"So?" She opened a bottle of water that was sitting on the coffee table. "This is the fourteenth floor. Like I said, you can't get up here without a special key card."

"You can if you want something badly enough."

She jerked her head back to him. "What do you mean?"

"Nothing." Lance didn't see any reason to tell her about what he'd just found. No sense in worrying her. He was here to protect her, not cause more stress.

"I'll sleep out here." He eyed the distance between the door to the bedroom she would be using. "On the couch."

"No you won't."

He ignored her and turned toward the line of massive windows. "I don't like this view either," he said as he reached to close the drapes.

"Wait. You don't like the *view*?"

"Correct. I don't like the view other people have of this suite."

She laughed. "There's no other building of this height for half a mile."

"I see that." Lance pointed to a building in the distance that was several floors taller than the hotel they were in. "But there's a perfect view from that building right there."

Ashley stood and walked over to the window, squinting. "No one can see *that* far." She looked over her shoulder at him. "Oh. Do you mean with like a telescope?"

"With a scope. Yes."

She turned all the way around and stared at him with her hands on his hips, her head tilted, eyes blinking. "Scope? You mean like on a gun?"

"Yes, I mean like on a gun."

She turned back to the face the window. "They can really see that far?"

"Easily. Snipers make shots farther than a mile all the time."

Ashley walked slowly back to the couch and sat down, letting out her breath as she did so.

"I didn't tell you that because I think anyone wants to shoot you." He noticed that her face had turned a bit paler. "I'm just saying it's easier to watch someone from a distance than you think."

She nodded, just as the phone on the coffee table buzzed.

Lance walked toward it, but Ashley leaped off the couch and reached it first. "Yes?" She scrunched her face into a ha-ha-I-beat-you look as she talked.

"Miss Hathaway, we have some flowers that were just delivered for you. Shall I have someone bring them up?" Lance overheard the conversation and shook his head violently, but she responded. "Oh, that would be lovely."

"Right away, miss."

"Why did you do that?" Lance scolded her as soon as she'd hung up. "You have to be more careful."

"Because it is what I would normally do." She stared at him with confident intensity. "You don't me want to raise suspicions by refusing flowers, do you?"

He stood there silently, not knowing whether to be angry

that she always had a comeback, or be glad that she was thinking about her own security. "Good idea," is all he said.

About five minutes later Lance heard a chiming sound.

"Oh, that must be the flowers." Ashley jumped up like an excited teenager, and ran for the door.

"Slow down," Lance ordered. He put his hand on his gun and looked through the peephole before nodding to her and stepping to the side, out of sight of the doorman. He was able to see the young man, who appeared star struck and shy, as he accepted the tip that Ashley gave him.

"Who are they from?" Lance followed her back into the living room where she sat the large bouquet on the center coffee table.

Ashley pulled the card out, and read the note. "Welcome to LA. See you soon." She turned the card over.

"Who are they from?" Lance asked again as he watched the color drain from her face.

"It doesn't say." She looked up at him and forced a smile. "Probably a friend of my father's."

Lance reached for the note and studied it. The handwriting was beautiful—probably done by the florist, not the sender. It was impossible to tell if there were evil intentions or not just from that simple missive—except that it matched word-for-word a missive he'd discovered on a bureau in one of the bedrooms.

"I'm going to put them over here." He walked toward the kitchen, and glanced back to see if Ashley was paying attention. She had relaxed into one of the chairs and was flipping through screens on her phone. Lance opened one of the large cabinet doors under the center island and shoved the flowers inside.

"Dammit," Ashley said.

Lance straightened up quickly, thinking she had noticed what he'd done. She was still staring at her phone. "What's wrong? Bad news?"

"I've been invited to the official meet and greet cocktail party at six o'clock."

"As in six o'clock tonight?"

She looked up at him with big blue eyes. "Yes. Sorry."

"But the premier isn't until tomorrow."

"I know. But it will look really bad if I don't go to this. Mrs. Wellington heard I was in town, and invited me."

"And who is Mrs. Wellington?"

"You need to get out more." Ashley shook her head. "She's the widow of Mr. Wellington. She's got more money than most countries, and enjoys throwing large parties and inviting important people."

When Lance didn't respond with anything more than a frown, she added. "There'll be an open bar and out-of-this-world appetizers."

"Oh, well then, by all means, we must go," he said sarcastically.

Ashley crossed her arms and pouted. "Don't blame me for this. I didn't know about it until just now—and frankly, there are a couple hundred other things I'd rather be doing than hearing the latest gossip at a cocktail party."

For the length of a heartbeat her eyes burned a brighter blue as her gaze roamed over Lance, giving him the impression that at least one of those things might involve him. She quickly restored her self-control, but that didn't keep Lance's thoughts from drifting as an explosive current raced through him.

It would be way too easy to forget this was an op, and get tangled up with this woman. Literally…tangled up…in the bed that loomed through the doorway just over her shoulder.

Yes, he'd seen the photos of her, and had known exactly what he was getting into. Yet he hadn't expected her to be quite so smart, or so alluringly authentic. And he certainly hadn't anticipated that she'd have the power to make a sensible man toss aside all reason and rationality.

Lance took a deep breath and willed himself to resist the urge to take her in his arms and satisfy his curiosity and longing.

"There's no way to get out of it," she said, interrupting his thoughts as she became businesslike again. "I'm going to hop in the shower and get dressed." She started walking toward her bedroom, but spoke over her shoulder. "There should be snacks in the kitchen and sandwiches in the fridge if you want anything."

"Thanks. I'll take a look."

She stopped when she reached the doorway, and turned halfway around. "Oh. I almost forgot. You have something appropriate to wear, right?"

"Of course."

Ashley nodded skeptically and disappeared.

Chapter 12

L ance walked around the penthouse again, checking every corner and door. The glass windows posed their own set of problems. Although the penthouse level was indeed higher than all the buildings near them, there was a building about a hundred yards away of equal height, and another about a half a mile away that was even taller.

A good pair of binoculars—or a riflescope—would make everything that happened in this room clearly visible. He stood with his hands on his hips and stared out at the landscape, his mind pondering the problem. When his stomach growled, he remembered what Ashley had said about the food, and headed for the kitchen.

The assortment of snacks, sandwiches and drinks was enough to feed two people for a week. Lance tried to eat lightly, knowing he'd want to sample some of the appetizers at the cocktail party later. He shoved a small finger sandwich into his mouth, and headed to the bedroom on the opposite side of the penthouse.

Pausing in the doorway, he shook his head in amazement as he studied the room again. It was larger than his entire apartment back east, and was tastefully and elegantly furnished with a king bed, as well as a seating arrangement of a couch and two chairs. A large cabinet, which he assumed held a large screen TV, stood against one wall that was decorated with gold trimmed wallpaper.

He walked toward the massive bed. *Too large to sleep in alone*, he thought as he swiped his hand across the luxurious pillows. Moving to the large closet, he took another look inside, exhaling with relief as he did so.

Colt had come through—or more likely, Caitlyn Madison, the wife of Colt's partner, Blake, had come through. In addition to the tux that he had seen when he did his first walk-through, there were two other ensembles of clothing hanging there. One was a suit, and the other, a less formal blazer and dress shirt.

He smiled as he thought about Caitlin and the behind-the-scenes work she did. *She* was the one who kept Colt and Blake in line, helping to make Phantom Force Tactical a highly successful and respected international agency. She'd gone from being a thorn in Blake's backside while working as an investigative reporter, to becoming his bride. Now, she handled tasks like this—the seemingly small, but extremely important details, like making sure Lance had the appropriate clothes for a mission.

Since the timeline on this op had been a bit fluid and hurried, he hadn't had time to pack the appropriate clothes. Okay. He didn't actually *own* the appropriate clothes. Caitlin had apparently gone shopping, and express shipped everything he could possibly need straight to the hotel.

Lance lifted the plastic covering and took a closer look at

his new clothes. The pair of slacks and suitcoat would work well for the cocktail party. The other collared shirt and the blazer would be perfect for any events that might spring up before the big premier tomorrow. On the other side of the closet, zipped up tight in its own plastic covering, was a tux.

Before hopping in the shower, Lance considered going to the ballroom to check everything out, but he didn't feel comfortable leaving Ashley alone. Instead he texted Colt, asking for some hotel floorplans, and went through the motions of spiffing up for a night in the public eye.

By the time he walked out of his bedroom later, Ashley was standing in the kitchen with the refrigerator door open.

"You clean up nice." Lance's eyes roamed over her. She wore a red dress that was tight across the waist and hips, then rippled down in soft waves to the floor. The dress was tastefully designed and conservative, yet accentuated a very athletic, slim, and feminine body. Her hair was held up in the front and side by combs, leaving the length of it cascading onto her shoulders and down her back.

"Not so bad yourself." The look on her face conveyed her thoughts even more so than her words, causing his heart to hammer foolishly. "How did you know I would be wearing red?" She stared at the red tie he was in the process of tying.

"Just a hunch," he said with no hesitation, and then paused for effect. "Actually, it's all part of the magical world of high-stakes security."

Inwardly, he was wondering the same thing. Somehow Colt knew everything, right down to what his client would be wearing. Maybe someday he would get Colt and Blake to share their trade secrets.

"Yeah, right." She popped a couple of grapes into her mouth, and then reached for something on the counter. "Do you think you could clasp this for me? I can never get these things to hook."

Lance looked down at the pearl necklace in her outstretched hand. "I'll give it a try."

Ashley turned her back to him and held up her hair. Lance took a step forward and tried not to stare at the creamy-looking skin of her neck as he drank in the sensation of her nearness. His hands began to tremble slightly as he caught the scent of her perfume, but he blamed his clumsiness on the clasp. "Why do they make these things so small?" he muttered.

"Can you get it?" When she tilted her head to the side to see if he was done, her body pressed against his even more. "What's taking so long?"

"Almost got it." By this time, Lance had indeed hooked the clasp, but he was enjoying the closeness too much to let it end yet. "Okay," he finally said, exhaling. "There it is. All done."

Ashley stepped away, and looked up at him curiously as if reading his mind. "Thanks." She walked over to a large mirror and checked her lipstick, then talked to him as she stared at his reflection. "You almost look like you do this all the time."

"So do you."

"Unfortunately, I've done it more often than I'd like." She turned to him with a slight frown. "Are you sure I look okay?"

He glanced at her, then away, so she wouldn't be able to read the *I-want-you* look in his eyes. "Yes. I'm sure you look okay."

"*Seriously?*" She tilted her head as she stared at him with her hands on her hips.

"Seriously *what?* Did I do something wrong already?"

"Yes. For your information, that is not a satisfactory answer to give a woman when she asks if she looks okay." She moved closer to the mirror, and turned left, then right, staring at her image with a displeased expression on her face. She fingered the necklace, and readjusted it, then lifted her gaze to meet his in the reflection again. "Maybe I should try on a different dress?"

"That one looks fine." He tugged at his tie. The room was suddenly very warm and the tightness of his collar felt like it was choking him.

"*Fine?* Are you *kidding* me? This is my first public appearance since my father passed away. It's the last movie premier he'll ever have. I need to look better than *fine*." She swung around to face him instead of talking to his reflection in the mirror. "Have you ever been around women before? Were you born in a cave?" She waved a hand in the air. "Never mind. Now I know why you're single—"

Lance walked toward her during the tirade, never removing his gaze from hers. He stopped when only about a foot away and ran the back of his fingers down her cheek. Since she was wearing four-inch heels, he didn't have to bend over, just tilt his head down a little. "Okay," he said, gazing straight into her blue eyes. "You look stunning." His voice was deep and gravelly. "Absolutely. *Stunning*."

He watched her throat convulse into a swallow, her eyes locked on his. "Th-thank you."

"And I'm single because the work I do doesn't allow much interaction with attractive, very sexy women." He allowed his eyes to roam downward, and then slowly back up. Her big blue eyes gazed innocently—and seductively—up at him. "Until now."

Her throat convulsed again.

Neither one said anything for a span of time that seemed to last an eternity. But both of them felt the emotion that simmered and flashed between them.

"Shall we go?" Lance held out his arm. It took every ounce of his strength to keep his focus on the mission—and every bit of resolve and willpower within him to resist removing everything she wore—except maybe the necklace, because that would take too much time.

Chapter 13

L ance carried on general conversation with Ashley
even as he was counting steps to the elevator and
surveying the layout of the hotel. He'd wished he'd
known about this cocktail party a little sooner so he could
have checked out the field of operation in more detail, but it
was too late to worry about that now.

"Do you think you'll have a good time?" Ashley's voice
interrupted his concentration.

Lance tugged at his tie. "Let me think about it…No."

"Why not?" She gave a sigh of exasperation, as he pushed
the button for the lobby. "You might find some of these
people interesting."

"Really? What do you think we have in common to talk
about? Football?"

She tilted her head. "No. I don't think that's a topic that
will come up."

"Target shooting?"

She shook her head violently. "No-o."

"The Constitution? Christianity?"

She hit him on the arm. "Hey, I'm just throwing some
options out there," he said innocently.

"Whatever you do, don't bring up politics or religion," she
hissed.

"So in other words, you're agreeing that I don't have much in common with these people."

"Neither do I, but I'm going to be nice."

"You have to be." He locked his eyes on hers. "I don't."

"Yes, you do. Number one, it's your job." She shook her head in aggravation. "And number two, you're my fiancé."

"And being your fiancé means I have to do everything you ask?" Lance's deep voice simmered with barely checked emotion, because his mind was busy visualizing things he hoped she would ask. He couldn't help but smile when he saw Ashley's cheeks blossom with emotion, suggesting to him that she was thinking the same thing.

Lance was just about to comment on it when the low buzz of conversation from the busy lobby area interrupted his train of thought, and the elevator began to slow down. Ashley stood close to the back of the conveyance, staring out at the crowd through the glass sides. Without warning, she gasped.

Before Lance could ask her what was wrong, she had grabbed the lapels of his jacket and pulled him to her. "Kiss me," she whispered.

Lance didn't ask any questions. He reacted accordingly, accepting it as his duty to respond to his client's request. Before the elevator came to a stop, he bent his head down to comply with her wish, assuming she had seen someone that needed to be convinced of their engagement. He expected to impart a gentle, dutiful kiss upon her lips—the kind a sophisticated fiancé would bestow upon his intended. He didn't anticipate that her arms would be wrapped around his neck, or that her leg would be pressed firmly against his.

And he didn't foresee that the spark that had been smoldering since they'd arrived in L.A. would suddenly burst into flame on an elevator. The gentle kiss that he'd planned became fiery and fervent as soon as his lips touched hers. Intense. Powerful. Lance had never experienced such evocative sensations in the mere joining of two lips before. For just an instant they were connected. One.

Perhaps it was all part of the attraction he'd felt from the first moment he'd met her. He worked hard to suppress the groan that rose from his throat when he heard the *ding* of the elevator doors opening.

Ashley heard it too. Breathless and red-faced, she released him, adjusted her gown and planted a nervous smile on her face before looping her arm into Lance's. "Thanks. That should have convinced him."

Lance looked around. "Convinced who?"

"*Him.*"

"Him who?" Lance could see she was flustered despite the look of regal calmness she wore on her face. "Tony?" He began to catch on. "He's *here?*"

She merely nodded while waving toward someone she knew on the far side of the room.

"Are you okay? Do you want to reconsider and go back to the room?"

Ashley took a deep breath and raised her head a notch. "No. I'm fine. Let's do this."

Lance appreciated her determination to go through with the event in spite of her obvious animosity and fear. He cleared his throat. "Do you think he saw you?"

She nodded. "He was watching us. Definitely."

"I hope we were persuasive enough." Lance paused and bent down so that he could whisper directly into her ear. "Maybe we should do it again to make sure."

His attempt to lighten her mood worked. The smile she shot him was small, but it was real—not the fake, ready-for-the-cameras look that she'd worn thus far when in public.

"I'd like that. Maybe later."

As his gaze traveled over her face and searched her eyes, something intense flared between them that caused his heart to kick. There was no sign of playfulness or joking in those big, blue eyes. Instead, they appeared alluring, full of seduction, reflecting desire and need. Even her words were suggestive, implying a proposition rather than mere assent. And did he imagine that her fingers pressed provocatively into his palm as she spoke?

He almost reached up to loosen his tie again. It was suddenly very hot and stuffy in the room, and the event had only just begun. It was going to be a long, hard night.

The ballroom lay straight ahead, and Lance braced himself for the flash of cameras and crush of bodies that he expected. He was surprised when none came.

"Did they ban the press in here?"

Ashley nodded. "Yes, they're very strict about that. There will be cell phone footage leaked out, no doubt, but this is a private party."

Lance sighed with relief. He didn't really want his face plastered all over the tabloids. From what he'd seen from the bits and pieces of local coverage on television, no one had gotten a clear shot of anything other than the top of his ball cap during his grand entrance into the hotel.

"I want you to tell me if you get any weird vibes from anyone." He looked down at Ashley. "Since we know Tony is here, we need to be on our toes at all times. Okay?"

"I will. Just don't go acting like a snarling big brother."

Lance's jaw stiffened. *Big brother, hell.* After that kiss, and the way she looked, he was going to find it hard to keep his hands off of her.

Even though there were no cameras flashing, as soon as they entered the room, Lance felt like he was in the receiving line at a wedding. They barely had the opportunity to move as people lined up to greet Ashley. He knew many of them had probably never met her or her father, yet pretended a lifelong intimate friendship.

Ashley was gracious and appeared relaxed, flawlessly introducing him over and over again just as they had rehearsed. Lance attempted to act relaxed as well, but his eyes were constantly moving, assessing, studying. In addition to the two large doors that opened to the lobby from which they had just entered, another exit lay on the far side of the room near the food tables. Caterers, wearing white jackets, were coming and going through that door.

Lance had studied the layout of the conference center on a map in the room, and figured that door probably led to a kitchen area.

"Yes, we are looking forward to the premier as well, aren't we, Jack?" The sound of Ashley's voice and the increased pressure on his hand, brought Lance back to the present.

"We've been counting down the days." He shot Ashley a smile and a wink, and started up a conversation with the man in the navy blue jacket, who seemed unable to keep his eyes off the woman Lance held at his side.

***

Ashley had to admit that she liked the feel of Lance's arm around her waist, but that only served to increase her anger. Mostly she was mad at herself for the way she reacted to him. It was bad enough that her heart felt like it was jumping out of her chest every time he so much as looked in her direction. But that kiss. *Je-zuz*. He'd made her melt right there on the elevator.

How dare he waltz into her life, take complete control, and try to protect her. She had been doing just fine without him. Smiling and accepting a glass of champagne from Lance that he'd lifted off a passing tray, she took a sip to calm her nerves, successfully controlling the urge to gulp it. *This is easy*, she told herself. *I've done it thousands of times.*

When Lance's hand slipped from her waist, Ashley found herself reaching for the protectiveness of his arm. It felt like a perfectly natural thing to do, yet she regretted the move as soon as she made it. *Too late*. Experience told her that a camera can pick up a split second of a facial expression or body movement and make it appear completely different from what was actually being felt. Despite the lack of media coverage, there were cell phones everywhere. She couldn't take the chance. She held on rather than pulling away.

"You okay?"

Lance's steady gaze bore into her in silent expectation,

sending an involuntary jolt of sensation through Ashley. It wasn't so much that calm, soothing smile that shook her as it was the intense look in his eyes—a look that bordered on smoldering desire. Her heart kicked at the bewildering web of attraction building between them.

Ashley hated to admit it, but she enjoyed having him by her side. She wasn't sure if it was the immense strength he exuded or the fact that the other women in the room couldn't keep their eyes off of him. Lance projected an energy and a power that enthralled her—and apparently every other female in the room. Just the nearness of him gave her comfort.

It didn't hurt that Lance's instant popularity also took some of the pressure off of Ashley. Yet she felt something strange boil up within her when she noticed the suggestive looks that women were throwing toward Lance. Most of them were much younger than she was, and many of them had flawless figures. Whether or not their attributes were natural or the result of numerous surgeries was a matter up for debate.

When Ashley glanced up to see if Lance was responding to the noticeable overtures from other women, it appeared he was oblivious. His eyes were constantly moving, assessing, studying. They weren't lingering or revealing any emotion. Either he didn't realize he was the hottest man in the room, or he was ignoring the fact that he radiated a vitality that attracted others like a magnet.

Out of the corner of her eye, Ashley saw a woman wearing a blue gown of shimmering sequins move toward them at a hurried pace. Her ample breasts seemed in peril of falling out of the gown with each step, giving the impression that she should have bought a dress at least another size larger. That spectacle alone made her hard to miss, but it wasn't the only thing that made her stand out in the crowded room. Perched on top of the gray hair piled high on her head was a small tiara that glittered brilliantly in the light.

"Be nice," Ashley whispered. "That's her."

"That's who?" Lance asked as the woman closed in on them.

Ashley didn't have time to explain.

"Why didn't you tell me?" A hand that glittered with diamonds grabbed Ashley's wrist. "I should be the first to know that you're engaged, and apparently I'm the last." She stopped talking and turned her attention to Lance, studying him over the top of her glasses curiously.

"Mrs. Wellington, I'd like you to meet my fiancé, Jack."

"Very nice to meet you, Jack." She gazed at him appraisingly now. "Ashley is like a daughter to me. I hope you take good care of her." Her tone was just a slight bit threatening.

Lance put his arm around Ashley's waist and pulled her close against him. "I intend to, ma'am. Thank you for inviting us."

Mrs. Wellington tilted her head as if listening for something, and then clapped her hands together. "There it is. I requested this song from the orchestra so that you two could have a nice slow dance together. At my age, I don't know if I'll make it to the wedding." She leaned in close. "When did you say it was?"

"You did wh—" Lance started to say, but Ashley already had him by the hand and was pulling him toward the center of the large crowd that had gathered. "We haven't set a date yet," she said over her shoulder. She stopped and put her hands up around Lance's neck, leaning in close. "Be quiet and act happy," she whispered into his ear.

Lance put one arm around her waist and pulled her even closer.

"Not *that* happy," she said through clenched teeth, while trying to smile and appear undisturbed.

Ashley felt Lance relax his grip a little, but she was still tightly ensconced in his arms as they began to move to the music. She forgot all else as he swept her across the floor with smooth, polished movements. There was suddenly nothing but the music, strong arms, and whirling lights.

Where had he learned to move with such ease, and from whom had he been taught to combine such immense strength with such gentle grace on the dance floor?

Ashley's mind wandered as she thought about the women Lance had likely held like this. She was reminded that this was a mission for him—just like hundreds of other missions. He was obligated to pretend he was enjoying himself, and was obviously quite experienced at performing any role assigned to him.

Although he had planted a smile on his face and appeared relaxed, she knew instinctively that Lance was aware of everything that went on around him. She felt the potent strength beneath her fingers that contradicted his unruffled composure and gentlemanly poise.

Lance was a professional. She knew he would do whatever was asked of him—and no more. He would do everything by the book. There would be no hanky-panky with this guy.

On one hand, it thrilled Ashley that Lance was a genuine, fearless, and charismatic man that could be relied upon. But on the other, she wondered what kind of spell he had cast upon her. She had never trusted a man other than her father. She'd never thought she would.

When the song was almost over, Ashley tilted her head up and spoke close to Lance's ear to make sure she wasn't overheard. "You're a natural actor here in Hollywood," she whispered. "It felt like you actually enjoyed that."

The song ended and they split apart, but only for a moment. Lance put his hand behind her neck and pulled her close, brushing his lips ever so slightly against hers as he gazed into her eyes. His look was so galvanizing it sent a tremor through her

He leaned his head close to whisper to her confidentially. "For the record, there was no acting involved."

Chapter 14

"Looks like you need another drink." Lance nodded toward her empty hand after they'd walked off the dancefloor.

"Okay, but no more champagne. Make it a gin and tonic." She paused as she appeared to reconsider. "Actually, just make it tonic water. I don't want to get tipsy."

"Why?" He smiled. "You don't trust me?"

She bit her lip, apparently to keep from replying, but he read the desire in her eyes, and knew it wasn't *him* that she didn't trust. That impassioned gaze, that yearning expression, was one that would cause most men to grab a woman by the hand and lead her to a place of privacy. Lance pushed all thoughts of doing such a thing aside, and searched over his shoulder to see if any wait staff were available. The open bars in each corner of the room appeared to be about five people deep.

Just then a group of three women appeared, and one of them took Ashley's hand. "Miss Hathaway, so glad you could honor us by attending. I was so sorry to hear about your father."

Ashley discreetly tilted her head in the direction of the bar as she struck up a conversation with the women, and added a slight roll of the eyes. Lance read the silent communication. This conversation was going to last more than a few minutes, and she'd changed her drink order back to a gin and tonic.

Lance walked the short distance to the bar, but kept his focus on Ashley and her surroundings the entire time. As the bartender prepared two drinks, Lance sent a quick text to Colt. *All quiet."* Then he pulled out his wallet and threw a bill onto the bar for a tip.

"Thanks, buddy." The bartender looked at it and smiled. "You need anything else, come back and see me."

Lance nodded and picked up the drinks, then headed back toward Ashley. In the split second he'd taken his eyes off her, she'd moved out of his sight, causing the hair on the back of his neck to feel prickly. After another few steps, she came back into his line of sight, right where he had left her. The group of women surrounding her had increased, which was why she had temporarily been hidden from his view.

But the prickly feeling didn't go away. Lance moved toward her, impelled by a nagging intuition at the back of his mind that refused to be stilled. His head began to swivel. He was alert; concerned, but not panicked. Something wasn't right. He didn't know what it was yet, but his Navy SEAL training and natural instincts had put his body on high alert, before his brain even understood the cause of danger.

Lance stopped where he stood, and took another note of his surroundings. Everything looked normal. Nothing out of the ordinary. The orchestra had just started a new tune, but it could barely be heard over the hum of conversation and the random sounds of laughter. He slowly let out a sigh of relief.

But that feeling of security did not last long. In the span of a heartbeat, his body kicked into high gear, and his senses were on high alert.

Ashley had noticed him and began waving to make sure he saw her. But at that instant, something else caught Lance's attention. Out of the corner of his eye, he noticed two men standing in the main doorway looking decidedly underdressed and out of place. They wore all black, including long bulky coats. He shifted his gaze to the man moving at a hurried pace out the door behind them. It was Tony Sturgis.

Lance began walking toward Ashley at a pace that caused the drinks to splash over the top of the crystal glassware. His eyes locked on hers as her expression turned to one of confusion at his urgent advance. Then her gazed moved to somewhere over his shoulder, and it took on a look of alarm. Lance dropped the drinks, cleared the last few yards in a flash, and grabbed Ashley. The sound of the glasses shattering on the floor hit his ears at the same time as the first distinct *pop* of a gun. The music stopped abruptly, and a loud voice spoke into the microphone. "Everybody get down! Stay where you are."

Some people in the room continued talking, while others laughed, apparently thinking it was some kind of joke put on by the movie production company. Most of the people stood frozen where they were, trying to make sense of what was happening before deciding what to do.

Lance didn't wait. He threw Ashley under the long row of tables that held the food. "Crawl as fast you can," he said, pushing her forward toward an exit door that seemed to be clear from any threats. He knew he only had seconds before it would be cut off by the men in black.

Lance cursed under his breath when his knee came down hard on one of Ashley's heels as she scurried on her hands and knees. Other people had begun to realize what was happening and began diving under the tables and lying down, slowing their progress. The chaos of people screaming, glass breaking, and the *pop, pop, pop* of gunfire made it feel like a bad dream.

Just seconds earlier, the room had been full of polite conversation, laughter, and music. Now it the only sounds were that of pure panic and fear, as those who had stood frozen and shell-shocked tried to find cover, or just hit the floor where they stood.

By the time most people came to their senses, Lance had pushed Ashley through an open door that led to an area where the hotel servers had been stocking the appetizers and punch. The staff must have fled at the first sounds of gunfire because the hallway was quiet and empty.

With a quick glance back, Lance counted three men who were in the process of closing all of the doors to the main lobby, preventing anyone from escaping. He knew it was only a matter of time until one of them concentrated on this side of the room.

The moment he closed the door behind him, he heard a man right outside. "No one through this door. Get down, now!"

As the yelling and confusion outside continued and swelled, Lance grabbed Ashley's hand and began running down the hallway. At the end of the corridor, he had a decision to make—left or right. With his gun in one hand, and Ashley's wrist in the other, he turned left, following a line of food carts that he hoped led to the kitchen. He pulled the door open with one swift move, and shoved Ashley through it. Then they both stood there staring at each other, breathing hard. They were standing in an employee restroom. Dead end. They were trapped.

Lance closed the door, pulled out his phone, and pushed a button.

"Is this really a good time to make a call?" Ashley asked. She wore no shoes now. Her hair was in complete disarray and the slit up the side of her dress was now a few inches longer.

Lance ignored her. "I have a situation," is all he said to whoever was on the other end of the phone. Then he slid it calmly back into his pocket.

Concentrating now on his next move, Lance looked around. The cubicle was about five by five, and contained a toilet and a sink. That was it—except for a mop and bucket along one wall, and a rack with hooks hanging on the other. Lance grabbed one of the white catering jackets that hung there. "Put this on. Take off your jewelry. Hurry."

Ashley hesitated a moment, then followed his order. After tearing off her earrings, she instinctively pulled her hair into a simple ponytail. As he stripped off his coat and grabbed a full-length apron from the array of kitchen attire hanging there, she rubbed off her lipstick with toilet paper.

"This should buy us some time."

He turned off the bathroom light, and placed the beam of

a small flashlight on the vent overhead. The panicked voices of those in the ballroom continued to reach them, increasing in both volume and intensity. Even from this far away, they could hear women whimpering, as some of the men in the ballroom tried to console them. In some cases, the men were the ones who seemed to need consoling.

"What are you doing?"

"Looking for a way out." He flicked the light across the grate. "And I think I may have found it."

"I'm claustrophobic," Ashley said.

"Too bad. It's the only way out. We're trapped."

Suddenly they heard footsteps approaching. Ashley turned to lock the door.

"No. Leave it unlocked," he whispered.

She glanced up at him with an expression of confusion, just as the footsteps increased in urgency and nearness. "They're coming." She mouthed the words, keeping her hand on the lock.

Lance nodded, then gently removed her fingers from the bolt. Maneuvering her behind the door, he pressed his back against her, and waited. He now had a decision to make. He could save his client by shooting whoever came through this door, or he could take his chances. The last thing he wanted to do was endanger the other hostages if a gun battle broke out.

Lance made the decision to keep his gun tucked away and leave both of his hands free. His plan was to rely on the element of surprise—if he had to—and to depend on his instincts to react to whatever happened.

As the footsteps drew closer, Lance discerned that it was

only one man. That helped reinforce his decision not to pull his weapon.

"Everybody out!" The shout came from a few feet away, followed by a fist banging on the door "Put your hands up, and you won't get hurt."

Lance felt Ashley take a long quivering breath, exhaling deeply so she could flatten herself against the wall even more. Lance tensed, ready to take whatever action was necessary.

The door handle turned, and began to open.

It seemed like minutes, but was mere seconds before the muzzle of a gun appeared and a hand reached in to turn on the light. Seeing only a toilet and a sink, the attacker backed out and yelled to someone else. "It's just a bathroom. All clear here."

"We need to find her," another voice said. "Remember, we need her alive, so she can tell us where it is."

Lance felt Ashley's legs begin to tremble and then outright shake. He turned and wrapped his arms around her as the footsteps receded, but his adrenalin was in overdrive now. This changed everything. Not only did she have something they wanted—but they knew she had it. This was turning into a mission that was much more complex than he'd imagined.

"It's okay," he whispered, running his hand down her back.

He waited a few moments, allowing her time to catch her breath. After the footsteps of the men had faded, he squeezed her to get her attention, which caused her fingers to tighten on his back. She stiffened, as if she anticipated what he was going to say, and her breathing stopped.

"Off-the-wall question here, but do you mind telling me what you have that they want?"

Chapter 15

Ashley knew this moment was inevitable. Why she hadn't told Lance sooner, she couldn't explain—not even to herself. At first, it was because she hadn't trusted him. But that was no longer the case. She believed in him. Relied on him. Had faith in him. And now, depended on him.

Entirely.

With her life.

Suppressing a sniffle that resulted from knowing how difficult this was going to be, Ashley slowly raised her head. He was staring at her impatiently. Irritably. She had jeopardized his life and the lives of all the others at the gala, because she'd wanted to do things her own way. It was time to come clean, and stop pretending that she could handle this on her own. She needed him. *Desperately.*

"Somewhere along the line, you *forgot* to tell me something." His tone was low and steady, but held a hint of anger. "Now would be a good time to *remember.*"

Ashley shrank from the look in his eyes, the distrust and disappointment in them—which hit her harder than the anger. A wave of nausea washed over her at his displeasure and regret. Maybe she had realized it too late, but there was no one on earth she admired more than Jarrod Landis. She wanted to see respect shining in his eyes when he looked at her—not regret. She focused her gaze away from his grim face and nodded.

"Yes. There is—"

A loud crash close by caused Lance to put his hand over her mouth to prevent her from answering. He pulled her into the circle of his arms, her face pressed against his wide chest. He stood silently for a moment, as he seemed to listen for a clue to what was going to happen next.

That's when the lights flickered and went out, causing a new wave of whimpering and screams from the ballroom.

***

More yelling and crashing of chairs and dishes covered up Ashley's answer, if she gave one.

Lance felt her shudder against him, and knew she was scared. His mind was already planning their next move. They weren't safe here. They had to stay one step ahead and keep changing their location. Any minute now, the terrorists would discover their target was not in the ballroom and would do another search—or one of them would need to use this restroom and discover that it wasn't empty after all.

Taking the intruders out one at a time—with his bare hands if necessary—was a plausible option. But there was a huge risk that hostages would be threatened if they didn't find what they wanted. Or *who* they wanted.

Lance knew that help was coming because of the call he'd made. The longer he could delay doing anything drastic, the better. The innocent people in the ballroom would fare much better if he waited on the launch of an organized rescue. This was not the time to be a hero. This was the time to hide and lay low.

"We need to go back down the hall and find the kitchen." He leaned in as close to her ear as he could. Even though his mind was busy working on their next move, he couldn't help but savor the smell of her. The feeling of her body pressed tightly against his was mind-numbing, but he forced himself to concentrate on the task at hand.

She seemed so small and fragile, yet, other than the slight trembling of her legs, showed little signs of fear. She wasn't bawling. Wasn't lying on the floor unable to move. He felt her nod against him and pull away slightly, while squeezing his hand. He took it as a sign that she trusted him, and was ready to move.

Pausing a moment, Lance put his hands on her face and touched his nose to hers. There were no words spoken in that inky darkness, but plenty was said. He knew she understood that he would protect her—with his own life if necessary. And the sound of a sigh on her lips conveyed that she trusted him.

Yet something else was reflected in that sigh as well. Determination. Resolve…And concern. The way she held onto him, her hands squeezing his arms, made it clear that any apprehension was not for her own wellbeing—but for his.

Lance gave his phone a quick glance before leaving the restroom, and saw a text message that read: *Eyes on ballroom. Five.* He couldn't help but breathe a sigh of relief. A team of ops had arrived and inserted a camera, confirming five bad guys. He texted back: *Heading to kitchen.*

He took her hand again, but stopped before opening the

door.

"What do you have that they want?" he whispered.

"It's a long story."

"Make it short."

"A key. To a lockbox."

"In L.A.? Why—" He stopped himself from asking why she hadn't told him sooner. It was a moot point now.

"I figured the fewer people who knew, the better." Ashely answered it anyway. "Dad's attorney sent it—just a key, with a note that said it went to a lockbox in L.A."

"Who else knows about it?" He opened the door and paused a moment, listening. Hearing nothing he squeezed her hand, letting her know they could continue.

"I didn't think anybody—other than the estate attorney."

"You should have told me," he whispered, moving ahead with his hand on the wall for guidance. "I was sent here to protect you. Remember?" He couldn't see her face, but her reply was little more than whimper.

"I didn't know who to trust."

Lance paused again to listen. They were almost to the hallway that they would have to cross to get to the kitchen. "Do you have it on you?"

"No."

That didn't make Lance feel much better. It only meant that if the bad guys were successful in capturing her, they would keep her alive until she told them where it was. What they would do to her to make her talk, he didn't want to think about. "Is it in the room?"

"In my left boot."

As they came to the "T" in the hallway, both of them stood with their backs flat against the wall and listened, knowing they would be making a run for it after this final pause. The hallway was dark and quiet as if the intruders felt confident they had checked this area and found it clear. The sounds of fear and the feeling of panic in the next room, on the other hand, had not lessened. They could be felt despite the distance.

"We're going to move fast. Don't stop running until I tell you to." Lance took a deep breath and gave Ashley's hand a squeeze to let her know he was ready to move. Then he took off at a dead run through the dark corridor, trying not to hit the food carts or make any more noise than necessary.

Lance knew the kitchen area had an exit door—he'd seen it on the floor plans. In the dim light, he made out the image of a door handle, just as the sound of footsteps and the voices of two men reached his ears from behind him.

"She has to be here somewhere. We saw her just before we entered."

Lance yanked hard on Ashley's hand, at the same time he opened the door. He pulled her through and closed the door in one motion, barely making a sound, but the men outside had stopped talking, as if they'd heard something—or sensed something.

Taking in his surroundings as quickly as he could from the dim light coming in through a window, Lance began to make his way toward a door on the other side of the room. The footsteps were approaching them now. They were loud, and were moving fast.

With his gaze intent on the door, Lance tried not to stumble or run into any objects in his path. *Slow is fast* he kept telling himself, though it seemed painfully slow, indeed.

He *had* to reach that door. And he *had* to get Ashely through it.

Lance had no fears or regrets about what he would face once she was safely out of the picture. He would be greatly outnumbered and vastly outgunned. The odds of making it out alive weren't in his favor, but he knew he could keep the attackers busy long enough for Ashley to get away.

That was his only objective.

Lance's breath came a little quicker now. He felt like human prey being stalked in the darkness, yet now the door handle loomed right in front of him, almost within reach. A smile actually reached his face as he stretched out and turned the handle.

The door was locked.

Chapter 16

Flashlight beams began bouncing back and forth across the room as the intruders found the door to the kitchen area. By then, Lance had pushed Ashley under a service cart and thrust his own gun into her hand before hurriedly placing a tablecloth over the top.

It was a last resort. They were trapped, and had only seconds left until the armed men were on them. Under normal circumstances, Lance would never part with his weapon, but the situation now appeared dire. He would go down fighting if necessary, but he had to give Ashley a chance. "Don't come out for any reason," he whispered, before quickly moving to the opposite side of the room. He hoped he could keep the intruders occupied—with his bare hands—so they wouldn't go searching for their real target.

The men were too close now for Lance to search for a hiding place, so he simply crouched behind a stainless steel food preparation island in the middle of the room. *Come on, Colt. Give me some backup.*

He heard the men standing in the doorway just a few feet away. "I'm sure I heard something in here," one said.

"Come out and we won't hurt you," the other one yelled, swiping his hand across a table of food and sending it sprawling onto the floor.

The men split up, walking toward Lance on separate sides of the counter. Sweat slid down his forehead as they drew closer. He had no weapon. Timing was everything. He waited until the one nearest him was just footsteps away. Then he stood and swiped his arm across the counter, sending a stack of pots and lids toward the approaching figure. The man was so startled by the sudden attack of stainless steel that he fell to his knees, his gun discharging haphazardly.

Before the other man could react, Lance grabbed a large butcher knife and hopped over the counter, dispatching the second man with a quick swipe to his throat. As that man fell to the floor, the other recovered his senses and began shooting again.

Lance pulled himself along the floor in the darkness in search of cover. *If I just had my gun.*

Suddenly there was a loud, sickening crack, and then a thump, followed by a *woomf* of air escaping. Lance picked up the flashlight that had rolled across the floor, and shined it over the counter. Ashley stood on the other side with both hands wrapped around the handle of an enormous cast iron frying pan. The gunman was lying at her feet.

Before he could scold her for coming out from cover when he'd distinctly told her not to—another man burst through the door. "Who are you shooting at? We need her alive!"

At the same instant, Lance heard his phone ding twice with a special ringtone. He yelled at Ashley. "Get down and cover your ears."

Ashley barely had time to react before the window along

the other side of the kitchen shattered. There was a loud bang, and smoke, and men pouring in through the broken glass, their guns concentrating on the last remaining intruder.

Then everything went silent.

***

Lance jumped up and ran toward Ashley, pulling her up into his arms. "You okay?" He gently brushed the hair away from her eyes.

She nodded, holding onto him with a tight grip. "I think so." She trembled as she stood staring at the tactical team who were moving methodically through the room like dark shadows, making sure it was secure. Some had come in through the window, while others had swarmed into the ballroom to surprise the other gunmen and protect the hostages.

"Did I kill him?" Her gaze drifted to the man lying stretched out on the kitchen floor, bleeding severely from a head wound.

"Probably not," Lance said calmly, "but I wouldn't want to have his headache when he wakes up."

"No bullet wound here that I can see." A man wearing tactical attire shined a light on the downed man, and then bent down and checked for a pulse. "What happened here?"

"Slugger here, cracked him over the head with a frying pan."

The man's face broke into a wide smile as his gaze slid over to Ashley. "He's kidding me, right?"

"I'm not kidding." Lance looked at her admiringly. "She saved my life."

"No." Ashley shook her head and swiped a tendril of hair from her cheek. "You saved *my* life. Here." She reached over to where she had hidden his gun, and offered it to him with a trembling hand. "I don't know how to use this thing."

"Doesn't look like you needed to." A medic signaled to someone over his shoulder with his flashlight. "We need to transport this one."

Just then the lights flickered and came back on, revealing a tall, broad-shouldered man approaching through the kitchen door. Like the others, he was dressed in black, yet he stood out as a leader among them. Black-gloved hands rested casually on a rifle that hung close to his body from a shoulder strap, as he paused and stared at Ashley.

The man never removed his gaze as he started across the room. Other members of the team instinctively moved out of his way, but whether it was from the intense look on his face, or the brisk, long strides that indicated a man on a mission, was hard to say.

"Rad?" Ashley's eyes were as large as the saucer cups on the stand beside her.

"Who did you expect? The tooth fairy?" The man's face broke into a large, relieved grin as he threw one arm around her and kissed her cheek. "You okay?" He wrapped both arms around her before she had time to answer, as if he needed to make sure she was all right by holding her close.

Ashley held onto him a minute, grateful to see another familiar face among all of the chaos, then pulled away. "Yes. Thanks to you."

Rad turned to Lance. "Hey, man. Nice to see you." He held

out his hand. "Thanks for taking care of things here. Good work."

Lance quickly wiped his sweaty hand on his pants and extended it toward the man, as Ashley watched in disbelief .

"Hey, Rad. Thanks for the help."

"Wait, you guys *know* each other?" Ashley's eyes darted from one to the other.

"We've talked on the phone a couple of times." Lance smiled mischievously.

Rad draped his arm over Ashley's shoulder in a brotherly fashion. "You don't think my buddy Lance here was going to take on a security op and not contact everyone he could about the job, do you?"

"You never told me you called Rad." Ashley looked at Lance accusingly.

"You never asked." He turned toward a police officer, and waved him closer. "Can you keep an eye on her for a minute?"

"Wait, but I—"

Lance put his hand on Rad's shoulder, walked a few feet away, and spoke in a low tone. "You find the key?"

Rad nodded. "There's someone waking up the bank manager right now. We'll know soon."

Lance glanced back at Ashley with an expression of concern. "Good. The sooner this nightmare is over for her, the better."

Chapter 17

I t took a few hours for the police to clear the scene, and for Lance and Ashley to finish giving their statements and answering questions. By the time they were given the go-ahead to leave, other pieces of the puzzle had fallen into place.

As Ashley sat with an officer in a small, quiet room away from all of the activity, Rad and Lance entered, both smiling grimly.

Ashley didn't speak. She just looked up questioningly… and hopefully.

Lance held out his hand to reveal a memory stick. "It's all here."

Ashley's gaze went from the small object in his outstretched fingers, back to Lance's eyes. "What do you mean?"

"Your father's work. The evidence. It's all here."

Ashley continued to stare, as if she couldn't understand what he was saying. She spoke, but continued staring into space, not at Lance. "It was in the lockbox?"

Lance nodded. "We only looked at a small portion of what's on this, but we saw enough to put Tony away for the rest of his life."

That statement made Ashley sit back down, hard. She swiped a hand over her face.

"For the murder of my father?"

Lance reclined into the chair beside her and took her hand in his. "His ties to organized crime are outlined in detail…so, yes, that makes a homicide case very feasible."

"And the fact that he sent men to find the key—at any cost—shows he is capable of anything," Rad said.

"How did he know about the key in the first place?" Ashley appeared calmer now, more in control.

"He paid a clerk in the attorney's office a large sum of money to tell him everything that was happening with your father's estate."

Ashley's eyes welled with moisture, but she didn't cry. "I don't know how to thank you for this."

"It wasn't just me." Lance glanced over at Rad and winked. "There was a lot going on in the background that you didn't know about."

Ashley looked up. "Like what?"

Rad sat down on the other side of Ashley. "Well, you know that flower delivery that came to your house every day?"

"Yes. What does that have to do with anything?"

"Well, Lance here told me to check it out."

Ashley's gaze bounced back and forth between the two.

"That was the first step in all this. Seems the flower delivery guy was under Tony's employ too. And those flowers had a listening device in them."

Ashley closed her eyes. "That's how he knew what I was doing."

"And what your father was doing." Lance rested his hand on her arm to comfort her. "Same with the ones that were delivered to the hotel room. I suspected something might be up, so I stuck them in a cabinet."

Ashley's brow wrinkled in confusion. "You did?" She sat staring into space, as if wondering how she hadn't noticed. Then she remembered the text she'd received, and how rushed she'd felt to get ready for the party.

Rad interrupted the conversation with a clap of the hands. "I think we're all done here. And you, young lady, need to get some sleep."

"Yes, we've been cleared by the police," Lance said. "Let's head up to the room."

A phone rang just then and the police officer on the other side of the room answered. "Sure thing. I'll tell them." He hung up the phone and turned toward Lance. "They executed a search warrant on Tony Sturgis's house."

"Hope they find something," Lance said.

"They already did," the officer replied. "And they just picked up Sturgis at LAX trying to leave the country."

Lance, Rad, and Ashley all exhaled at the same time.

"Then I guess our work here is done." Lance turned to Rad and shook his hand. "Thanks for your help. Hope we get to work together again in the future."

"Likewise. Say hi to Colt for me…and tell him we're even." Rad shot him a sly smile and then tilted his head toward Ashley. "Take good care of her, okay?"

Lance's brow wrinkled questioningly at the look Rad had given him. "I will."

Ashley seemed a little dazed and overwhelmed, so he took her by the hand and led her the short distance to the elevator.

Neither spoke as they entered the conveyance, and even as they ascended, the only sound was the dinging that marked the different floors. Lance put his arm around Ashley's waist as the door opened, and guided her to the room.

Once inside, he walked straight to the liquor cabinet and poured a glass of the amber fluid, which she accepted with shaking hands.

"You okay?"

"I think so." Taking a sip, she closed her eyes as the liquid ran down her throat. "At least I'm better than I was." She paused and stared at him. "I can't thank you enough for being here and putting up with my…"

He closed the short distance between them and lightly touched her mouth with his finger. "I didn't have to put up with anything. I enjoyed your company."

The statement made her smile. "No you didn't. You couldn't have. I acted like a spoiled, ungrateful child." She thought about it a minute. "Then again, I guess that's probably what you were expecting."

Lance pursed his lips as he thought about it. "To tell you the truth, yes—so you weren't as bad as I thought you'd be. In fact, there were times when this mission was almost enjoyable."

"*Almost?*"

She stared up at him with a look that stole his breath away. Lance couldn't speak for a moment as he studied her face. It seemed softer now, relaxed, and serene. But there was something else in those glittering eyes, he couldn't quite decipher. Was she scolding him for using the wrong word again? Or was there something more intense and passionate burning there?

The image of their passionate kiss in the elevator flashed through his mind just then, along with the comment she had made afterward. Had he seen an invitation in the smoldering depths of her blue eyes? Or had he only imagined it?

"I know I don't deserve it, but could you give me a second chance?" Ashley's voice was like a whisper, sounding soft, sexy…and seductive.

Unable to remove his gaze, Lance noticed that the expression she wore had changed once again, and was no longer hard to decipher. Her eyes were big and blue. Her lips were pink and parted. And her expression had changed to one of longing and desire.

Lance raised his brows, and tried to appear unaffected by the sudden heat racing through him. "Second chance?" He cleared his throat when the words came out huskily. He could usually count on his self-control—it was one of his strengths. But suddenly the one woman he shouldn't want was the one pushing his willpower to its limit.

She nodded and ran a single fingertip up his chest toward his buttoned collar. "If you'll give me a second chance, I'll try to prove to you that I can be better than…*almost* enjoyable."

Lance studied her hand breathlessly as it moved up his shirt. The room grew hushed with words unsaid, and everything began moving in slow motion. When she got to the top, she slid the button through the hole with a smooth, fluid movement, releasing the tight collar. The choking sensation Lance had felt all evening was instantly relieved, but at the same time, the pressure running through his veins hit a new intensity.

He instinctively took a deep breath, before his gaze went back to hers. He tried to remain calm and keep his voice level and businesslike. "I never questioned the fact that you *could* be..." He cleared his throat. "Ah...enjoyable. But I have a strict personal rule about getting involved with clients."

He attempted to conceal the fact that he was exceedingly close to throwing his rule out the window; that his fingers ached to reach out and touch her. He'd never been this attracted to a client before. Hell, he'd never been this attracted to a woman before. Every neuron in his body seemed to be on fire as he tried to restrain himself and remain professional.

"The mission is over. I'm not your client." Ashley took his arms and placed them around her waist, then wrapped her own around his neck. "Right?"

Lance closed his eyes so he could think without staring into the seductive blue orbs staring back. The mission *was* over. He'd been cleared by Colt to go home. Theoretically, he could get on a plane right now and fly back east. He'd only agreed to stay because it was late, and he'd thought he'd try to get some shuteye. That, and Ashley had invited him to fly home on her jet rather than book a commercial flight.

Her arms increased their pressure and drew him even closer. "Don't you want to find out *how* enjoyable?"

Lance's breathed escaped him in what was almost a groan. He leaned forward, enjoying her boldness and the feel of her body pressed close to his as he nuzzled his face in her hair. "It's late," he murmured, trying to reason with her, while still holding on to his last bit of self-control. "Don't you want to go to bed?"

"That's what I'm trying to tell you." She turned her head and pressed her lips hungrily against his, verifying that this was an invitation, not a mere suggestion.

Lance enjoyed the heat of her skin pressed against his and the taste of her mouth as he explored it with his tongue. But taking a deep breath, he pulled away slightly again. "This changes everything," he whispered, lightly kissing her neck and shoulder. "I'll never be able to work for you again."

"I understand." Her voice was soft and suggestive as the hot breath of her kisses pressed against his cheek. "You'll only be able to work *with* me."

Lance smiled as he lifted her into the cradle of his arms and carried her toward the bedroom. "That sounds like an offer I can't refuse."

Epilogue

One year later.

A shley stood on the porch, her hand resting on the railing as she watched the work being done on a row of cabins about a hundred yards away. In the opposite direction, birds of every size and color chattered and sang around feeders hanging randomly in a line of trees.

The sun, bright and hot on her face, added to the overall warmth she felt. It gave her a great feeling of accomplishment to be fulfilling her father's dream of expanding his foundation for veterans to now include a sanctuary and retreat. She had known he was an avid supporter of the military because of his devotion to the foundation he'd created, but it wasn't until after his death that she'd found his plans for a veteran's refuge. It had all been laid out in an easy-to-follow blueprint.

Every goal. Every obligation. Every dream.

And now, a warriors' retreat was coming to life right before her eyes. Already the rooms in the main house were full of men who needed a little time to relax and unwind from a deployment before returning to their homes and civilian life. A new row of private cabins was being built for those who wanted a little more privacy, and a central meeting place with a large fire pit had been created and tastefully landscaped.

A sigh escaped her as she studied all the work that had already been completed. Construction workers had just built a long dock at the lake, and boats and canoes were sitting on the shore waiting for anyone who needed some quiet time on the water. The barn and pastures were full of horses again, a large gym had been built, and a gun range was in the works.

Ashley was just about to turn and go back inside when a familiar figure emerged from the shimmering sunlight in the distance, his boots raising a cloud of dust with every step. He was sweaty and dirty, and had just emptied a water bottle over his head to help cool him down. Following close at his heels was Garth.

When he got to the bottom step of the porch, he looked up at her with a grin, water still dripping out of his dark wavy hair, causing his snug tee shirt to cling to his body.

"What're you up to?" he asked.

"Waiting for the sexiest man on earth to take a break."

Lance grinned. "You mean the dirtiest."

"I've been working in the barn and grooming horses, so we can debate who's dirtier."

Lanced hopped up the remaining steps and threw one strong arm around her waist before pulling her tight against him. "We can hire someone to do that, you know."

"Yes. Just like we can hire someone to do *that*." She nodded toward the construction site he'd just left.

"I want it to be right," he said, staring pensively at the cabins.

"You mean you want it to be *perfect*."

He nodded, still staring into the distance. "Nothing is too

good for my brothers."

The look on his face made Ashley's eyes well with tears. Her father's dream had become Lance's dream the minute he'd heard of it. He was committed. Dedicated. It had become his top priority.

Ashley felt a wave of pure happiness wash over her. It pleased her that she could use the money from her father's estate for a good cause. She didn't need the material things that her wealth could provide—and more importantly, she didn't want it.

All she wanted was here. No glitz and glamor. No gossip or bitter feuds between people trying to climb their way to the top. No bright lights or crowds. Ashley had never been more content or grateful for the direction her life had taken her. She relished the peace and quiet that surrounded her, and savored every minute working by Lance's side.

"Don't worry," Lance said, interrupting her thoughts. "Once everything is up and running, I won't work such long hours."

"Yes you will." She threw her arms around his neck, and kissed him on the cheek to let him know she wasn't mad.

He eyed her sheepishly. "Well, it won't really be *work*."

She sighed. "That's true. Once we get everything up and running, it won't seem like work at all. It will be my dad's dream come true."

Lance took her by the shoulders and held her at arm's length so he could look into her eyes. "And yours."

She nodded. "And *yours*."

He sighed deeply, pretending to be distressed. "But by then

you'll probably be tired of having me around, and want to fire me."

"*That* could be a problem."

"Why?"

"I can't fire my own husband, can I?"

"Good point." He laughed and bent down for a kiss. "And good planning on my part."

"No." She ran one hand through his hair, while pulling him down for another kiss. "Good planning on *my* part."

BONUS MATERIAL!

KEEP READING FOR A SNEAK PEEK OF FINE LINE! (Phantom Force Series Book 2)

CONNECT WITH THE AUTHOR

Email Jessica@JessicaJamesBooks.com
BookBub: bookbub.com/authors/jessica-james
Amazon Author Page: www.amazon.com/-/e/B001IYTXOG
Goodreads: goodreads.com/author/show/586216.Jessica_James
Facebook: facebook.com/RomanticHistoricalFiction
Twitter: twitter.com/jessicajames
Pinterest: pinterest.com/southernromance/
LinkedIn: inkedin.com/in/authorjessicajames/

About the Author

JESSICA JAMES is a multi-award winning author of historical fiction and military suspense. Her novels appeal to both men and women, and are featured in library collections all over the United States, including Harvard and the U.S. Naval Academy.

By weaving the principles of courage, devotion, and dedication into each book, she attempts to honor the unsung heroes of the American military—past and present—and to convey the magnitude of their sacrifice and service.

Dear Reader

I am honored that you took the time out of your busy schedule to read this book. If you enjoyed the journey, would you consider sharing the message with others?

Write a review online.

Recommend this book to friends in your book club, church, school, workplace, or class.

Go to facebook.com/romantichistoricalfiction and "like" the page. Post a comment about what you enjoyed most.

Mention this book in a Facebook post, Twitter update, Pinterest pin, or blog post.

Pick up a copy for someone you know who would be impacted by the story—or send a copy to a soldier serving our country.

Visit the author's website at jessicajamesbooks.com and sign up for the newsletter to keep up on giveaways, new releases and special events.

Check out my other award-winning books!

Other Books by Jessica James

AWARD-WINNING ROMANTIC SUSPENSE
DEADLINE (Phantom Force Tactical 1)
FINE LINE (Phantom Force Tactical 2)
FRONT LINE (Phantom Force Tactical 3)
MEANT TO BE: A Novel of Honor and Duty

AWARD-WINNING HISTORICAL FICTION
THE LION OF THE SOUTH
SHADES OF GRAY: ANNOTATED
SHADES OF GRAY: A Novel of the Civil War in Virginia
NOBLE CAUSE (1 Military Heroes Through History)
ABOVE AND BEYOND (2 Military Heroes Through History)
LIBERTY & DESTINY (3 Military Heroes Through History)
HEROES THROUGH HISTORY BOXED SET (Books 1-3)

HISTORIC NON-FICTION
FROM THE HEART: LOVE LETTERS FROM THE CIVIL WAR
THE GRAY GHOST OF CIVIL WAR VIRGINIA

Praise for Jessica James' Books

"Very engaging. Hard to put down."
— BILLY ALLMON
U.S. Navy SEAL (Retired)

"Sweetly sentimental and moving… An endearing page-turner."
— PUBLISHERS WEEKLY

"Expertly crafted from beginning to end. A truly extraordinary read."

— MIDWEST BOOK REVIEW

"A tapestry of emotion deeply set inside the bravest of Americans: the soldier."
— MILITARY WRITERS SOCIETY of AMERICA

"Reminds me of *American Sniper* and *Lone Survivor*, but accompanied with a beautiful and epic love story that is completely unforgettable."
— LAUREN HOFF
United States Air Force

Jessica James Awards

2017 IndieBRAG Medallion Winner

2016 Gold Metal Military Writers Society of America

2016 Readers' Favorite International Book Award

2016 BOOK OF THE YEAR Finalist/Foreword Magazine

2015 NJRW Golden Leaf Award

2014 Valley Forge Romance Writers Sheila Award Finalist

2014 John Esten Cooke Award for Southern Fiction

2014 Reader's Crown Award Finalist

2014 Next Generation Indie Award Finalist in Fiction/Religious

2013 USA "Best Books 2013" Finalist in Fiction/Religious

2012 Bronze winner Foreword Magazine Book of the Year in Romance

2011 John Esten Cooke Award for Southern Fiction

2011 USA "Best Books 2011" Finalist in Historical Fiction

2011 Next Generation Indie Award for Best Regional Fiction

2011 Next Generation Indie Finalist in Romance

2011 Next Generation Indie Finalist in Historical Fiction

2011 NABE Pinnacle Book Achievement Award

2010 Military Writers Society Award in Historical Fiction

2009 HOLT Medallion Finalist for Best Southern Theme

2008 Indie Next Generation Award for Best Regional Fiction

2008 Indie Next Generation Finalist for Best Historical Fiction

2008 IPPY Award for Best Regional Fiction

2008 ForeWord Magazine Finalist for Book of the Year in Romance

BONUS MATERIAL

FINE LINE (Book 2)

Blake Madison reached for the alarm at the first ding so it wouldn't wake his wife.

"It's Saturday," Cait said sleepily, reaching for his arm. "Sleep in."

"I'm going for a quick run." He crawled out from under the covers, carefully moving Max's head off his legs. "It's a lot of pressure having a young trophy wife. I have to stay in shape."

She threw a pillow at him, but then reached over and ran her hand over his abs. "You're doing a pretty good job of staying in shape."

The comment made Blake smile. He had gotten back into a weightlifting and running routine shortly after getting married, and was in almost as good a shape now as he had been when he was a young Navy SEAL. Then again, Cait was pretty fit herself. She had taken over most of the barn chores, and actually enjoyed splitting and stacking wood. She was always amused when other women saw her toned arms and requested the contact information for her personal trainer.

Dressing as quietly as he could in a pair of sweatpants and

tee shirt, Blake headed toward the door.

"You forgot something," he heard from beneath the covers.

He went back and bent over her. "I know. But I was afraid I'd be tempted to crawl back into bed."

"Good answer." She reached up, grabbed a handful of his shirt, and pulled him down for a kiss, causing him to linger.

Sitting on the side of the bed, he leaned down with his hands propped on each side of her pillow. "Do you know how much I love you, Mrs. Madison?"

She grinned sleepily and pulled him close again. "Show me."

"I just did that a few hours ago. Remember?"

"Umm hmm." She drew the words out with her eyes still closed and a contented smile on her face. "But that was last night."

He glanced at the door, then back at the bed.

She must have sensed his hesitation. "I'm just kidding. We have all day. Go for your run."

Blake lifted her hand off the covers and kissed it. "We've been married almost a year. We need to start acting like an old married couple, not newlyweds."

"Are you saying you want me to become a nag?"

"Only if you nag me about getting back into bed with you."

He gave her another long kiss, and then stood and stared down at her in the dim light. She was wearing his NAVY tee shirt—or as she called it, her favorite negligée—with one arm lying on top of the blankets. His gaze fell on her wedding band, and then drifted to her tousled hair spread out on the pillow and her long lashes resting on her cheeks. He reconsidered his need for outdoor exercise.

"Bring me a cup of coffee when you get back," she murmured, pulling the covers up and rolling over.

"I won't be long, baby." He headed toward the door and patted his leg for the dog to follow. "I'll take Max so you don't have to get up and let him out."

"Love you."

His heart flipped. "Love you more."

Just as he started to close the door, she spoke again. "Don't miss me too much."

He grinned as the door clicked shut. She always said that when he left, even if they were only going to be separated for a few minutes. It had become a routine. Even the kids said it now when they left for school or went to visit a friend.

Heading down the stairs he turned off the security alarm and went out onto the porch, taking a deep breath of the cool morning air. After doing a couple of stretches, he sprinted down the lane with Max trotting along beside, his heart bursting with happiness and contentment.

These early morning runs were as much for his mental wellbeing as for physical training. He usually used the time to clear his mind and focus on his business goals for the day. But as he listened to the cadence of his feet hitting the dirt road and the sound of his steady breathing, his mind drifted to his upcoming anniversary instead. He wanted to come up with something really special to celebrate—something that would show Cait how much she meant to him and the kids. It had been on his mind for weeks, but now the milestone moment loomed just days away and he still didn't know what that something was.

Moving to the side of the lane to avoid a large mud puddle, his mind continued to drift and wander. He thought back to the day he'd proposed, causing the vivid memories to replay through his mind like a movie.

Cait had just finished testifying at a congressional hearing about Mallory and Senator Wiley, and was waiting for him by the Washington Monument. He'd snuck up behind her and grabbed her around the waist with one hand and the shoulders with the other. Drawing her up against him, he'd whispered in her ear. "Come here often?"

She'd tried to turn around and look up at him, but he held her firmly with her back pressed against him. "If that's your best pick-up line, you're going to be a lonely man," she'd said.

"Really? It works in the movies."

"Sorry. But, no."

"Okay. How about this?" He'd leaned down and whispered in her ear. "Hey, baby. Wanna ride in my truck?"

"Now you sound downright creepy," she'd said. "That's a definite no."

"Okay. Let me see... Close your eyes this time."

"All right. They're closed."

"Hey, sweetheart." He had let go of her then and backed away. "Are you free?"

"I don't know." She'd laughed, but continued to stand with her back to him. "When?"

"The rest of your life."

Whether it had been his words or the seriousness of his

tone he didn't know, but she'd turned around with a perplexed expression on her face—and found him down on one knee, with Drew on one side and Whitney on the other. All three held onto a sign that said, Will you marry us?

Blake smiled at the memory. Her surprise and the children's pure delight at being a part of the occasion had forged a memory he would never forget as long as he lived.

Bypassing the security gate and turning left at the end of their long driveway Blake continued toward the main road, his breath coming faster now and creating short bursts of steam in the chilly morning air.

The gate made his thoughts wander back still further, to when he and Cait had testified against Senator Wiley and Mallory. They'd tried to keep a low profile and return to their private lives, but the media attention and social media campaigns from political fanatics made that impossible. There had been lots of intimidating communication and a few death threats immediately following the scandal, so despite the home's isolation, Blake had taken the extra steps of installing an electronic gate to stop vehicles, and upgraded the security system in the house.

The addition of Max and the fact that his house was a sort of informal headquarters for his security firm, made him feel pretty secure and confident that his family was protected. There was rarely a day when at least one former Navy SEAL did not stop by or spend the night—and depending on deployments for his company, there were often half a dozen or more.

Blake inhaled the musty smell of dying leaves and contemplated the gold and red colors splashed like a painter's canvas all around him. It was Cait's favorite time of year, and was beginning to be his as well. They'd harvested the last of the vegetables and pumpkins from the garden, and spent any free time together stacking wood in preparation for the coming winter. Somehow it wasn't work when Cait was involved. It was pure pleasure.

Passing the two-and-a-half-mile mark he knew by heart, Blake slowed down. The image of Cait lying in bed turned him around before he'd made it to the main road. If the kids were still asleep, maybe he'd take a quick shower and re-join her.

Sprinting the last hundred yards, Blake was surprised when Max didn't follow him up the porch, but continued around the side of the house with his nose to the ground. The dog usually had a pretty hearty appetite after a run and wanted fed immediately.

"Where you going, boy? Smell a raccoon or something?"

Blake let him go and entered the house to find Whitney walking slowly down the stairs, looking disheveled, but looking wide awake. So much for going back to bed. "What are you doing up so early, young lady?"

He didn't hear her answer as he continued into the kitchen to make a pot of coffee. With the coffee starting to brew, he stood in the glow of the open refrigerator door, trying to figure out what to make for breakfast. Maybe he'd surprise Cait with breakfast in bed as an early anniversary gift.

Whitney shuffled into the room behind him and noisily pulled out a chair at the small kitchen table. "When is Cait coming back?"

"What, honey?" Blake continued staring into the fridge. Having just turned four, Whitney talked a lot, but didn't always make sense.

"When are they going to bring her back?"

Blake closed the refrigerator door slowly as a twinge of dread crawled up his spine. He turned to Whitney and knelt down beside her. "What men, honey? What are you talking about?"

"The mean ones that came." Her eyes brimmed with tears.

Blake didn't ask any more questions. He stood and turned in one movement.

Racing to the stairs, he took them two at a time and headed at a full sprint down the hallway to the master bedroom. He tried to open the door quietly, hoping to find Cait still sleeping, but he almost tore the door off its hinges in his urgency.

The bed was empty.

Order FINE LINE (Book 2) today!
Available wherever books are sold!

Visit www.jessicajamesbooks.com

www.ingramcontent.com/pod-product-compliance
Lightning Source LLC
Chambersburg PA
CBHW022021170626
46808CB00003B/1017